A SILENT KILLER

He moved forward and saw the man seated with his back to him. This would be Lee, the man he'd paid to give him information and to leave the door open. The man moved closer to Lee, reached out, and grabbed the long, braided tail of the unsuspecting man's hair. He yanked back on it, bringing Lee's chin up sharply, exposing his throat. The man switched his hand from the braid to cover Lee's mouth. He saw the fear in the Chinaman's eyes just before he sliced Lee's throat with his blade . . .

DON'T MISS THESE
ALL-ACTION WESTERN SERIES
FROM THE BERKLEY PUBLISHING GROUP

THE GUNSMITH by J. R. Roberts
Clint Adams was a legend among lawmen, outlaws, and ladies. They called him . . . the Gunsmith.

LONGARM by Tabor Evans
The popular long-running series about U.S. Deputy Marshal Long—his life, his loves, his fight for justice.

SLOCUM by Jake Logan
Today's longest-running action Western. John Slocum rides a deadly trail of hot blood and cold steel.

WITHDRAWN

THE GUNSMITH

180

CHINATOWN ASSASSIN

J. R. ROBERTS

JOVE BOOKS, NEW YORK

CHINATOWN ASSASSIN

A Jove Book / published by arrangement with
the author

PRINTING HISTORY
Jove edition / December 1996

The Putnam Berkley World Wide Web site address is
http://www.berkley.com/berkley

ISBN: 0-515-11984-9

A JOVE BOOK®
Jove Books are published by The Berkley Publishing Group,
200 Madison Avenue, New York, New York 10016.
JOVE and the "J" design are trademarks
belonging to Jove Publications, Inc.

PRINTED IN THE UNITED STATES OF AMERICA

10 9 8 7 6 5 4 3 2 1

THE GUNSMITH

180

CHINATOWN ASSASSIN

PROLOGUE

The rain made different noises in the night. The sound it made when it struck the tops of the canvas tents was singular, except where the water had pooled. Then it just made splashing sounds, as it did in all the muddy puddles in the street.

This end of Dodge City was made up largely of tents and rickety wooden shacks. The section that the man was walking through was Chinatown. Here a man could gamble and find a Chinese whore or pipe. It was dark and deserted at almost four a.m., and the man moved through the streets as quietly as he could. The mud sucked at his feet and, he sometimes thought, at his soul. There was a fire in his breast that had to be quenched, and this was where he always came to quench it. Most towns of any decent size had a Chinese section, or a China*town*. Men were often found in unguarded moments here, whether in the arms of a woman or the thrall of a pipe. He knew that the man he was looking for would be floating through opium-induced dreams by now. He had paid enough money to be notified the next time he showed up in Wong Foo's opium den.

The man moved from the street into the tented areas of Chinatown. The sound of the rain striking the canvas over his head was oddly soothing. The boardwalk here was dry now. After having soaked up water from the bottoms of countless boots, enough time had gone by for it to dry out. He moved soundlessly over the walk until he reached Wong Foo's establishment. A wooden, two-story structure, it was the best crafted of the poor lot. Wong Foo's was the only building that could survive a stiff wind, the man was sure.

He had to step into the rain again, ankle-deep in the mud, to move around to the back door. As promised, it had been left ajar. He'd paid enough for that, as well.

He opened the door, slipped inside, and closed it behind him. He knew that most of the men inside would be too lost in their euphoria to be aware of his presence. Still, he moved quietly, leaving behind wet and muddy footprints. That was alright. He wasn't trying to hide the fact that he'd been there. By morning everyone would know that.

The air around him was musty and pungent. He wondered if he stayed inside long enough if he'd start to feel the effects of the opium. Probably not. It needed to be drawn deeply, directly from the pipe, to have its desired effect.

He paused and waited for his eyes to adjust to the dimness. Ahead of him he could see the individual fires of the oil lamps, kept low. They were not for light, but to be used on the long-stemmed pipes so that Wong Foo's customers could simply roll over on their pallets, extend the pipes to the flames, and inhale.

He moved forward again and saw the man seated with his back to him. This would be Lee, the man he'd paid to give him information and leave the door open. He was dressed traditionally, in what looked to white men to be pajamas. The man moved closer, reached out, and grabbed the long, braided tail of the unsuspecting man's hair. He yanked back on it, bringing Lee's chin up sharply, exposing his throat. The man switched his hand from the braid to cover Lee's mouth. He saw the fear in the Chinaman's eyes just before he sliced Lee's throat with his blade. Whatever sound Lee made was muffled by the killer's hand. Blood flowed down over the dead man's chest, and the killer eased him from his chair to the floor.

Next the man moved in among Wong's clientele. He eased from pallet to pallet silently until he came to the right one. He looked down at his quarry, a white man whose eyes were fluttering, showing only whites through the slits of his eyelids.

The killer took the time to look around him at the others who were lying in the pipe's arms. The only person who could have identified him was Lee, and he was taken care of. None of the others would ever be able to point him out, even if they were able to see him.

He looked back down at his target, lying totally helpless on his back. He placed the palm of his hand beneath the man's chin, exerted pressure to expose the throat, and then used the already bloodied knife to slice from ear to ear.

Clint Adams looked up from his breakfast and saw Sheriff Bat Masterson approaching him. The grim look on his friend's face made him put his fork down and sit back in his chair.

"What?" he asked as Bat reached him.

Bat sat down heavily across from Clint.

"Another one last night."

"Chinatown?"

Bat nodded.

"Who?"

"Axle Johnson," Bat said. "His throat was cut while he was lying in a crib at Wong Foo's."

Clint made a face.

"I didn't know Axle took to the pipe."

"I didn't either. One way or another, that's a deadly habit to take to."

"Any witnesses?"

Bat shook his head.

"A Chinaman was also killed, the same way."

"Throat cut?"

Bat nodded.

"That's three," Clint said.

"I know."

Bat looked around Delmonicos and saw some of the patrons looking over at him.

"People are expecting me to do something," he said. "I'm not a damn detective, Clint."

"I know," Clint said. "They're just scared."

"All they have to do is stay out of Chinatown."

"I guess they're afraid that the killer won't stay in Chinatown," Clint said. "What if he comes into this part of town?"

"If he does," Bat said, "I'll catch the son of a bitch, Clint."

"I know," Clint said, "I know you will, Bat."

But he had his doubts. . . .

ONE

San Francisco
Six Years Later . . .

Clint looked up from his hand and stared at the face of the man across the table. The other three players had dropped out, and now it was just between the two of them.

"It seems you have an interesting hand," Jason Birch said to Clint.

Clint smiled.

"At least as interesting as yours."

They'd been playing draw poker in the Alhambra for three hours now, and between them they had most of the money on the table. When he first sat down, Clint felt that Birch had the edge, because he played poker for a living. At best, Clint considered himself a talented amateur, although others—like Luke Short and Bat Masterson—considered him to be much more.

A crowd had gathered around the table, because the

5

pot was a big one, having swelled due to the game's no-limit raise rule.

Clint had been in San Francisco for a week, doing nothing but playing cards and meeting women. Occasionally, he tried some other games of chance and, in fact, had won quite a bit during a run of luck at the roulette table. He had hit a number with ten dollars on it—just passing time—and then let the almost two-hundred-dollar winnings ride, and hit again.

"It's your bet," Clint said. He had just raised a hundred dollars, which had forced the last of the other players from the game. It was the fourth raise.

Birch made a show of looking at his cards, but Clint knew that was the man's style. Good hand or bad, Birch made a show of studying his cards. He had kept three, and drawn two. Clint figured him for three of a kind before the draw, and he had probably improved to either a full house or four of a kind.

Clint knew that this was an unusual hand, and he had to play it to the hilt.

"Call your raise," Birch said, "and raise two hundred."

Definitely four of a kind, Clint thought, looking at his own cards.

"This could go on all night," he said, "so I'll just call."

He felt he had the losing hand, but he couldn't fold so he tossed in the last raise.

"Full house," Birch said, laying the cards down, "kings over."

He had three kings and two tens.

Surprised, Clint laid down his four threes. He'd felt that a low four of kind was going to lose this hand.

"Four threes."

Birch sat back and mock applauded.

"Well done," he said. "Gentlemen, I think I'm done for the night."

"So soon?" one of the other men asked.

Birch smiled, collecting his money.

"I have other pleasures to attend to."

Clint checked the time and saw that he, too, had to call it a night—as far as poker was concerned.

"You guys are leaving winners," another man said.

Birch smiled and said, "I thought that was the point of the game."

"Yeah, well . . ." the man said.

"You'll get your chance to get it back," Clint said, collecting his money.

As he and Birch walked away from the table, the other man said, "Buy you a drink?"

"Sure," Clint said, and they went to the bar.

"I thought you had that last hand," Clint said when he had a beer in his hand.

"So did I," Birch said with a shrug. "I played it wrong. It happens."

They sipped their beer.

"Your mind must have been elsewhere, Jase," Clint said. "I've never known you to play a hand wrong."

"You mean you've never known me to admit to it," Birch said. "Yes, my mind is elsewhere."

"Other pleasures?"

"Yes."

"I'm meeting a woman myself shortly."

"Good for you, Clint," Birch said. He raised his glass and said, "Here's to other pleasures."

Clint acknowledged the toast.

"Well," Birch said, putting his empty mug on the bar, "I'm off. See you tomorrow?"

"I'll be around," Clint said.

"Good," Birch said. "I need to make up for that last hand."

Birch left and Clint checked his watch, saw he had time for another beer, and ordered it. His "other" pleasure was named Patricia Chase and he was to meet her in half an hour down the street at the Jack of Spades, Portsmouth Square's newest hotel and casino.

He wondered what Birch's "other" pleasures might be. The man seemed to have studiously avoided mentioning whether it was a woman or not. Did he have another game set up? Or was he going to cultivate some other interest? He'd only known Birch a few years, having seen him on and off on perhaps three occasions during that time. He certainly had no idea how many vices the man might have, or what they might be.

He decided not to dwell on Jason Birch's vices, but to tend to his own. He would finish his beer and then mosey down to the Jack of Spades a little early so he could look it over before meeting with Patricia Chase.

TWO

The Jack of Spades had all the modern conveniences, including some electric lights. The casino was easily the largest in the Square, and Clint wandered around observing the games, placing a bet here and there, wasting time until Patricia arrived.

Patricia Chase was a visitor of San Francisco. She was an artist from New Mexico who had come to California to try to "awaken her vision." She had found herself growing stale at home and thought a trip might do her good.

They had met on her second night in San Francisco, and he had offered to show her around. They spent the next day together, and then the night. This would be their fourth night together, and she was leaving the next day.

Clint finished touring the casino and went out to the

lobby to wait for her to arrive. They were going to have dinner in the Jack of Spades dining room.

When she arrived she looked beautiful in a red gown that was off the shoulder, revealing her creamy shoulders and cleavage. She had very black hair that had a gray streak, even though she was only in her early thirties. She wore her hair up, and the gray streak was very prominent.

They kissed briefly, cheek to cheek, in the lobby and went into the dining room together.

"I want this to be a special night," she told him. "My last night here."

"We'll make it special," he said.

"Would you order for both of us?"

"Sure."

The waiter came over and Clint ordered from the menu for both of them—steak dinners, with all the trimmings.

"I have meat-and-potatoes tastes," he told her, because there were many other things on the menu, including lobster and snails—two things he would never eat.

"That's fine with me," she said.

Over dinner she told him that she would like him to come to New Mexico so she could paint him.

"Me?"

"Yes," she said. "You have striking bone structure in your face, which you probably didn't have five or six years ago."

He touched his face and said, "You mean I'm getting old."

"Older," she said, "and we all are, and our faces are the better for it, I think. Do you think you would come?"

He smiled and said, "It's possible, Patricia."

"But you won't promise, huh?"

"I hardly ever make promises," he said, "so I don't have to break them."

"That seems like a sound practice."

After dinner they had dessert—peach pie and coffee—and then he asked her if she'd like to gamble.

"I don't think so," she said.

"Then what would you like to do?"

"I think you know."

"Take a last walk around town?" he teased.

"No."

She reached across the table and took his hand.

"Don't tease me."

He squeezed her hand and asked, "Your room or mine?"

They went to his room and made love, slowly at first, and then lay in each other's arms.

"This has been very good for me," she said.

"What?" he asked. "This?" He moved his hands.

She jumped and said, "Yes, that too, but that's not what I meant."

"I know."

"I meant the whole trip, especially you. I'm ready to go home now and paint the things I've seen."

"Really? I haven't even seen you sketch anything. I thought artists started with sketches."

"Well, I have a secret to tell," she said. "I have sketches in my room. I'll be taking them home with me and using them as the basis for some paintings."

"Really? Do you have any sketches of me?"

She hesitated, then said, "Yes."

"I'd like to see them."

"Oh, I don't think so."

"Why not?"

"Well, they're very rough, and besides, they're in my room and we're not going to go to my hotel to see them now, and I'll be leaving in the morning—"

"All right, all right," he said, cutting her off. "I won't insist on seeing them. Will you be painting me from them?"

"I might, but nothing would be as good as a live model."

He thought she was going to start asking again if he'd come to New Mexico to be painted, so he turned his head and kissed her.

"Is that your quaint way of telling me to shut up?" she asked.

"No," he said, rolling her onto her back, "this is my quaint way of telling you to shut up."

He moved down and kissed her belly, then moved lower, using his tongue and his lips. He found her wet and fragrant, and as he pressed his lips to her he reached beneath her to clutch her buttocks and lift her to him. His tongue entered her and she gasped.

"How am I . . . to keep quiet . . . if you're going to do . . . that!"

He didn't answer, and she didn't keep quiet.

THREE

When Clint came downstairs the next morning it was after nine a.m. Patricia had awakened him earlier by slithering down between his legs and paying special attention to a part of him that quickly responded. She took him in her mouth and lovingly sucked on him until he exploded, lifting his hips up off the bed and stretching his arms out over his head.

"You're not so quiet either," she said, laughing, kissing the inside of his right thigh.

"Jesus," he said, "who could keep quiet when you do that?"

He'd watched her dress then. She had just enough time to go to her hotel, change, and catch her train.

"I could come and see you off."

She placed her hand over his mouth and said, "Don't. I hate good-byes at train stations." She removed her hand from his mouth and kissed him. "I'll see you when you make it to New Mexico."

"Sure," he said, again making no promises.

That had been at seven-thirty, and he had fallen asleep and awakened an hour later, feeling oddly refreshed.

He was staying at the El Camino Hotel, on Montgomery Street, because a friend of his had recommended it. While not up to the standards of Portsmouth Square, it was certainly better than any hotel he'd ever stayed at in any western town. As an extra added bonus it had free newspapers in the lobby for its guests, and he picked up two—the *Chronicle* and the *Morning Call*— to read over breakfast.

He carried the two newspapers into the dining room and ordered his usual breakfast of steak and eggs, and coffee.

"Biscuits today, Mr. Adams?" the waiter asked.

"Why not?"

He'd very much enjoyed the company of Miss Patricia Chase of New Mexico while it had lasted, but now that she was gone he'd be able to concentrate more on other matters—like poker. Of course, that was only if he was able to avoid the company of another young lady during the rest of his stay.

He read the *Chronicle* over breakfast and opened the *Call* while he had his second pot of coffee. Some of the stories were the same, but the *Call* came out earlier, so it had a story that the other paper didn't, one that caught Clint's attention.

"GAMBLER KILLED IN CHINATOWN OPIUM DEN!" the headline announced. He read further and discovered what Jason Birch's other pleasure had been the night before. Not a woman but a pipe, a pipe that had apparently turned out to be deadly.

"While in the thrall of opium, Jason Birch's throat

was cut, leaving him to bleed to death, a fact which went unnoticed for some time. . . ."

Clint read the rest of the article quickly, absorbing the salient points and then lowering the newspaper.

"Sir?"

He realized then that the waiter had been talking to him.

"What? I'm sorry, did you say something?"

"I asked if you'd be needing anything else?"

"Oh, no, nothing," Clint said. "Thank you."

"Is there anything wrong?" the man asked.

"Just some bad news in the paper," Clint said.

Clint sat back, staring at his half-filled cup of coffee. Granted, he'd only seen Birch a few times over the past two or three years, but he considered the man a friend. He was going to have to find out something about what happened last night.

The last time Clint had been in San Francisco he'd gotten involved with a Japanese man who was seeking his emperor's sword. Remarkably, through all of that, he had managed to avoid contact with the police. This trip, however, it didn't seem possible.

He picked up the newspaper again and looked to see who had written the article on the death of Jason Birch. The byline said: Allan Marks. He decided he would first check with Marks before going to the police.

FOUR

If Clint remembered correctly, Mark Twain had once worked on the *Morning Call*, back in 1864. He was sure Twain had told him stories about that time during one of their meetings.

As he approached the building that housed the *Call*, he also recalled that the paper had only been seven or eight years old at that time. Now, twenty years later, it was more firmly ensconced as a part of San Francisco's legendary newspaper community, although certainly not of the stature of the *Chronicle* or the *Herald*.

He presented himself at the city desk and asked for Allan Marks.

"Who wants him?" the man behind the desk asked. He had not even bothered to look up from his desk while asking.

"My name is Clint Adams."

The man's head came up quickly and Clint knew that he had recognized the name.

"Don't go 'way," the man said. "Stay right there and I'll get him for you."

"I'll stay here," Clint assured him.

The man went off, but not before looking behind him a couple of times to make sure Clint hadn't moved. Finally, he disappeared from sight, but hurriedly returned with a second man in tow. The second man looked to be in his early thirties. He had his white shirtsleeves pushed up over his forearms and a pencil behind one ear. Who else could this be but Allan Marks.

"I understand you claim to be Clint Adams," he said, appearing less impressed than the first man.

"I don't claim to be anybody," Clint said. "Is there some reason you shouldn't believe me?"

"Well, you'll forgive me, Mr., uh, Adams, but we get a lot of people up here claiming to be someone they're not. I had somebody here earlier in the week claiming to be Bat Masterson."

"Bat's not in San Francisco."

"I found that out later, but only after wasting some time on him. So you can see where I'd like to be careful."

Clint stared at the man.

"Would you like me to shoot someone to prove who I am?" he asked finally.

"That won't be necessary," Marks said. "All I'd need is a reference."

"Here in San Francisco?"

"That would be nice."

Clint thought a moment. His habit of staying in different hotels each time he came to town made it difficult ... but he thought he knew a couple of people who would do the trick.

"Check with Duke Farrell at the Farrell House Hotel, and Peter Styles at the Clapton House."

"You know these gentlemen personally?"

"Yes," Clint said, "they'll vouch for me."

"I'll look into it," Marks said. "Why don't you come back with me."

"Don't you want to check me out first?"

"Both of those names you gave me are not generally bandied about," Marks said. "If you're willing to use them as references, I'm inclined to believe you are who you say you are."

Clint stared at the man for a moment and then said, "I could shoot a cigarette out of your mouth or something."

Marks shuddered and said, "I don't think that's necessary. Besides, I don't smoke. Why don't you follow me."

"Sure."

Clint trailed behind the man until they came to a large office.

"Yours?"

Marks shook his head.

"My editor's, but he's out today, so we can use it."

They went inside and closed the door behind them. Marks sat behind his editor's big mahogany desk and looked comfortable.

"What can I do for you, Mr. Adams?"

"I'm interested in the story you wrote for today's early morning edition."

"The murder in Chinatown?"

"That's the one."

"Why?"

"I knew the man who was killed."

"Jason Birch."

Clint nodded.

"How did you know him?"

"I played cards with him a few times."

"Was last night one of those times?"

"Yes."

"Did he say he was going to Chinatown last night?"

"No," Clint said. "He just said he had to deal with other pleasures."

"Well, I guess to some men opium is a pleasure."

"What happened?"

"There isn't much more to tell that wasn't in the paper," Marks said. "One of the Chinamen found him in his crib, lying in his own blood. He'd been dead awhile."

"Someone got in and out without anyone seeing him?" Clint asked.

"Apparently it's not that difficult."

Something had been nagging at the back of Clint's mind ever since he'd read the article, and when Marks mentioned Bat Masterson it had been knocked loose.

"Is this the first?"

"The first murder in Chinatown?" Marks asked. "Hardly."

"No, I mean the first one like this," Clint said.

"Like what? In an opium den?"

"A white man," Clint said carefully, "seeking pleasure in Chinatown."

"Seeking pleasure . . . hey!" Marks sat forward. "Have you seen this kind of thing before?" The reporter took the pencil from behind his ear and grabbed a pad from the desk top.

"Yes."

"Where?"

Clint, who'd been standing up to that point, sat down opposite Marks.

"Dodge City."

"When?"

"About six years ago," Clint said. "You reminded me of it when you mentioned Bat Masterson, because Bat was sheriff then and he had to deal with it."

"With what?"

"Several white men were killed in Chinatown in Dodge City," Clint said. "In the Chinese whorehouses and opium dens."

"White men seeking their pleasures in Chinatown," Marks repeated.

"Yes."

"And the killer was the same?"

"Nobody knows."

"He wasn't caught?"

"No," Clint said. "He just . . . stopped."

"After how many were killed?"

Clint thought a moment.

"I believe it was four."

"In what period of time?"

"It's not real clear in my memory," Clint said, "but I think it was a matter of weeks, maybe a month."

"Three weeks to a month," Marks said, writing. "Were they all killed the same way?"

Clint nodded.

"Their throats were cut."

Marks kept writing.

"I seem to remember at least one innocent bystander killed, as well. A Chinaman from the opium den."

Marks continued to write, then stopped and put the pencil down. He sat back in his boss's chair.

"Mr. Adams, do you have any reason to believe that this is the same killer?"

"None at all," Clint said. "In fact, I didn't even think of it, immediately, not until you mentioned Bat."

"Then why did you come here, originally?"

"Because I knew Jason Birch, and I wanted to see if there was any more information."

"I don't have anything further to add," Marks said. "Some person or persons unknown killed Mr. Birch by cutting his throat while he was all but unconscious."

"Who is the policeman handling the investigation?"

"His name is Inspector McGowan."

"Will he talk to me?"

"Maybe," Marks said with a shrug. "Lord knows he won't talk to me, but you're not a member of the press and, after all . . . you *are* Clint Adams . . . aren't you?"

FIVE

Clint hadn't learned much from Allan Marks, but Marks had managed to jog his memory about the Dodge City Chinatown killer.

As Clint remembered, that killer had almost cost Masterson his job when he suddenly just . . . disappeared. *That* had driven Masterson even more crazy, because he had vowed to catch the man. Now, six years later, had the same killer surfaced in San Francisco? If so, what had he been doing for the past six years? Had he done the same thing somewhere else? How many towns had a Chinatown? Clint knew that Sacramento had one, and places like New York and Denver.

On the other hand, maybe it wasn't the same man, and maybe this wasn't the first in a string of murders. Maybe this was an isolated incident and Jason Birch had simply been unlucky.

Clint went to the police station from the offices of the

Morning Call, determined to offer what he knew and let Inspector McGowan do with it what he would.

Inspector McGowan turned out to be a portly man in his late fifties, who seemed to have little interest in what Clint had to offer.

Clint asked to see the man when he reached police headquarters and within ten minutes he was shaking the policeman's rather chubby hand. Not only was it plump, but the man offered it limply. They spoke right there in the lobby of the police station.

"I knew Jason Birch," Clint said.

"Birch?"

"The man who was killed in Chinatown last night."

"Ah, yes," McGowan said, nodding, "Birch. Too bad, what happened."

"Tell me, Inspector, was he robbed?"

"As a matter of fact, he was not," McGowan said. "He still had his wallet on him, and there was quite a bit of money in it."

"He had won at poker last night," Clint said.

"I see."

The fact that Birch had not been robbed was also in keeping with the Dodge City victims.

"I expect you'll want to bury him," McGowan said.

Clint immediately felt bad, because he hadn't even thought of it.

"There's no family in San Francisco, is there?" the policeman asked.

"No, sir," Clint said. "As a matter of fact, I don't know if there's any family anywhere, so you're right, I will want to bury him."

"I'll have the body released as soon as I can."

"Thank you."

"If that's all . . ."

"Actually, Inspector, I didn't come here about burying my friend," Clint said, "I came with some information, perhaps about who killed him."

"You know who killed him?"

"No, but I know that this kind of thing has happened before."

"Mr. Adams, men are always being killed in Chinatown," McGowan said. "Sometimes it's over a woman, sometimes a gambling debt—"

"I'd just like to tell you what I know," Clint said. "You can decide what to do with it."

McGowan, looking put-upon, shuffled his feet, said, "Very well," and left it at that.

Realizing he was not going to be offered a place to sit, Clint started to tell the policeman about Dodge City, six years earlier. The man listened impatiently, several times looking pointedly at his pocket watch. Clint was losing steam along the way, realizing that the man was probably going to do nothing with this information— and why should he? It probably meant nothing.

"So this man was never found?" McGowan said when Clint finished.

"No, he wasn't."

"Well, it's a very interesting story, Mr. Adams, but at the moment we only have one dead body, not several. There's no reason for me to believe that this was anything but an isolated incident, another in a long line of Chinatown killings."

"You're probably right."

"I'm experienced, Mr. Adams," McGowan said, "and because of that I am often right. Will there be anything else?"

"No, I guess not."

"I'm sorry about your friend, sir," McGowan said.

"Where are you staying? I will notify you when the body can be picked up."

Clint told him what hotel he was in.

"Will you be in San Francisco much longer?"

"I had intended to stay another week, at least."

"Well, I hope nothing else will happen to keep you from enjoying the rest of your stay."

"I hope so, too, Inspector."

Clint left the police station feeling foolish. He'd been treated with something less than respect, and in fact had simply been tolerated. He did not even know if the policeman had recognized his name when he introduced himself.

He decided to go back to his hotel and see what he could find out about an undertaker. Also, he'd check the register to see what Birch had put down as his home, and then see if he could locate any family.

None of this was what he had had in mind for the remainder of his stay in San Francisco.

SIX

The killer watched Clint Adams leave the police station, just as he had watched him leave the offices of the *Morning Call*. When he had first seen Adams at the Alhambra, playing poker, it had all come back to him. Suddenly, it was six years ago, and he was back in Dodge City. The only thing that would have made it perfect was if Bat Masterson was also present.

The killer followed Clint Adams back to his hotel. He was fairly certain he knew how to lure Bat Masterson to San Francisco. If he could accomplish that, then they could continue the game they had started in Dodge City.

He thought back to last night, the very moment he had slit Jason Birch's throat. He'd experienced a feeling of power that he had not felt for some time. He had managed to fight off the urge for six years—had kept that particular beast at bay all that time—but seeing Clint Adams had brought it back full force. He wondered

26

what Adams would think when he found out that he was actually the cause of his friend's death.

After all, it was Clint Adams's presence that had unleashed the beast once again, wasn't it?

SEVEN

Several days passed before Clint was notified at his hotel that Jason Birch's body could be picked up and "disposed of." During that time he had checked with the law in New Orleans, where Birch was originally from, looking for family and finding none. He felt bad that the man had no family, but then neither did he, and he was managing just fine. At least he didn't have to pass on the bad news to a wife or mother.

He also watched the newspaper each morning, reading very carefully for news of another murder, but if another one was forthcoming, it was probably too soon.

And then there was the uncomfortable feeling that he was being watched. It could have been the police, keeping an eye on him, or even someone from the newspaper.

It could also have been a killer.

He'd been a bystander in Dodge City, offering Bat Masterson as much moral support as he could, but there was really never anything for him to actually do. Bat was the law, and he was a visitor, but certainly the killer must have known he was in town. What if the killer was here in San Francisco and had spotted him? It seemed likely, since he'd chosen Jason Birch as his victim. If he had seen Birch, then he had seen Clint.

Clint had gotten the name of an undertaking firm from the hotel and he asked the hotel to notify them to pick up the body.

"Yes, sir," the clerk said. "We'll see to it."

"Thank you."

"We will let you know when the undertaker has the body."

Clint nodded and walked away from the desk. As he did he noticed a man entering the lobby and recognized him as Allan Marks, from the *Morning Call*.

"Mr. Marks," he said, as the man reached him. "Looking for me?"

"As a matter of fact, I am," Marks said. "Could we sit down someplace, maybe have a cup of coffee? I'll buy."

"How about the dining room?" Clint asked.

"That's fine."

They went in, were shown to a table, and ordered a pot of coffee.

"What can I do for you, Mr. Marks?" Clint asked when they each had a full cup.

"Do you read our paper every day?" Marks asked. He had noticed that Clint was carrying two newspapers, and had placed them on the table. One was the *Chronicle* and the other the *Call*.

"They're given out free in the lobby," Clint said. "So I read them."

"Oh, I see."

"What was it you wanted to see me about, Mr. Marks?"

"Well, I was wondering, since you're planning to be in San Francisco for a while longer—"

"Who told you that?" Clint asked.

"Well—"

"Inspector McGowan?" Clint asked. "He was the only one I told."

"Well, yes, I did speak with the inspector after you did."

"To check on me or to follow up on the murder?"

"Well, both, actually."

"And how did he react to what I had told him?"

"He thought it was a bit far-fetched."

"And what's your impression of the inspector?"

"I'm afraid the inspector and I don't have much use for one another," Marks admitted.

"Is that because he's lazy?"

"Lax would be a better word," Marks said. "The inspector has been on the job a long time, and I think he'd like to coast into retirement."

"What do you think he'll do if there's another murder?" Clint asked.

"I have a better question."

"And what's that?"

"What will you do if there's another murder?"

"What should I do?"

"Well, you'd be the only person in this city with any insight into the killer."

"I have no insight—"

"You were there, in Dodge City, when the first murders were committed."

Clint studied the younger man.

"You did some research, didn't you?"

"I looked at some of the old Dodge City newspapers

from the time," Marks said. "Bat Masterson did not seem to know quite what to do, did he?"

"Bat's a lawman, Mr. Marks, not a detective."

"I've done some research into your past, too, Mr. Adams," Marks said. "Looking beyond the obvious, I see that you have acted as a detective a time or two, and with some success."

"I'm no detective."

"More of one than Bat Masterson, I'd wager," Marks said, "and probably more of one than Inspector McGowan, as well."

"Why did you come here today, Mr. Marks?"

"I was wondering if you'd agree to an interview—"

"I don't do interviews anymore, Mr. Marks," Clint said. "I've had too many bad experiences with reporters putting words in my mouth."

"You'd have approval—"

"I've heard that before."

Marks frowned.

"I see I'm being penalized for my colleagues' past indiscretions."

"Somebody had to be," Clint said. "Sorry."

"That's all right," Marks said. "Are you still planning to stay awhile?"

Clint stared at him.

"That wasn't an interview question," Marks added hastily, "just my own curiosity."

"I'll be staying until the end of the week," Clint said. "I'll probably be burying Jason Birch tomorrow or the next day."

"No family?"

"None that I could find."

"Too bad."

"Maybe not," Clint said. "At least he's not leaving behind any grieving mothers or widows."

"That's one way to look at it, I suppose," Marks said. "Well, thanks for your time."

Marks stood up, but Clint decided to remain and finish the coffee.

"Thanks for the coffee," he said.

"Sure. I'll be seeing you."

Clint watched the reporter leave and wondered how he'd feel if he left town at the end of the week and then heard that there'd been another murder. But if he stayed in town and waited, how long should he give it? A week? Two? He couldn't afford to sit and wait to see if the killer would indeed strike again.

Who was he kidding? He had no appointments, no pressing engagements. His life had become a series of trips east, and west, north and south, without much purpose—and that was fine with him. At his age why couldn't his purpose just be to enjoy life?

Which brought him back to staying or going. Neither one would put him out any, or anyone else for that matter—except maybe the killer.

EIGHT

The killer watched the man walk down Ross Alley, his arm around the little Chinese girl. No whorehouse for this fellow, no sir, just a good ol' Chinatown doorway or crib. This kind of thing was usually seen on the Barbary Coast, where whores plied their trade wherever they could. The killer figured this man was requesting this kind of tryst, which—in the killer's mind—made him even more twisted than most of the men who sought their pleasures in Chinatown.

The killer was no prude, not at all, but there were certain things decent men could not abide.

He followed more closely than he might have, but neither the man nor the girl were noticing. They were too busy with each other. In fact, the way they were walking he was sure the girl had her hand down the man's pants.

It was late and there was hardly any moon. They were

in Ross Alley, and it was even darker there, because it was all shadows. The man and girl finally found a doorway they liked and stepped into it. The killer knew then that he was going to have two victims this night, not just one.

He waited a few minutes. When he heard the two people moaning he started to move toward the doorway. When they came into view, he saw the man standing with his trousers down around his legs, and the Chinese girl crouched down in front of him. The man's head was thrown back, making it easy for the killer to simply step forward and slice his throat with his knife.

Blood gushed down over the man's chest and down onto the girl. For a moment she didn't know what was happening. It was too dark for her to see what the wetness was, but it was sticky and she apparently knew the smell of blood.

She looked up at the man's face and was about to scream. The killer took one step and kicked her in the side of the head before she could make a sound. He hadn't noticed before, but her dress was down around her waist, exposing her small, naked breasts. He leaned over her, a smile stretching his face tightly, and went to work with the knife. . . .

NINE

Clint started the next morning with the *Morning Call*. He wanted to see if Allan Marks had fashioned some sort of interview out of their conversation yesterday. It was over his first cup of coffee that he saw the story of the second murder. This time a Chinese girl had been involved, and she'd been killed, too. Not only killed, though. She had been mutilated.

"Jesus . . ." Clint said, lowering the newspaper and shaking his head.

"Sir?" the waiter asked. "Is there something wrong?"

"Yes," Clint said, "there is something very wrong."

"Do you still want your breakfast?"

Clint looked up at the waiter.

"Got to start the day with a good breakfast, right?"

"Yes, sir."

"Bring it out."

The extent of the girl's mutilation was not reported in the newspaper. If it had been, maybe he wouldn't have had his breakfast after all.

Clint found it odd that the killer had struck the day after Allan Marks had asked him what he would do if the killer struck again. Clint had hoped it wouldn't happen again, or if it did that he'd be far away and not hear about it.

No such luck.

And no such luck that he wouldn't be involved, because just after he finished his breakfast Inspector McGowan entered the dining room, looked around, spotted him, and started toward him.

"Mr. Adams."

"Inspector," Clint said, "what can I do for you?"

"May I sit?"

"Please."

McGowan sat and saw the newspaper on the table.

"I see you've read the paper."

"If you mean the story about the murder, yes," Clint said. "I saw it."

"Tell me," McGowan said, "when you encountered this, uh, sort of thing before, were there any, uh, innocent bystanders killed?"

"Yes," Clint said, "a Chinaman was killed."

"Was he mutilated?"

"No, but then he wasn't a woman, was he?" Clint asked. "Was this girl a prostitute?"

"Yes."

"Where did it happen?"

"Ross Alley."

"*In* the alley?"

"In a doorway."

"What was the extent of the mutilation?"

McGowan hesitated and looked around, to see how close the other patrons were.

"He cut off her breasts."

Clint stared at the man.

"And took them with him."

Clint closed his eyes.

"Do you think this is the same man?" McGowan asked.

"I don't know, Inspector," Clint said. "The man in Dodge City never killed a woman."

"Then maybe this was his first."

"I hope it's his last," Clint said, but somehow he doubted it. This killer, whether he was the same one or not, seemed to be getting bolder if he took the time to cut the girl's breasts off right in Ross Alley.

"It must have happened late," Clint said, "when the alley was empty."

"That's what I figured," McGowan said. "I'm going to have to go to Chinatown and ask some questions."

This sounded to Clint like the man was going to have to do his job, finally.

"Why don't you talk to Nok Woo Lee?"

McGowan stared at Clint for a few moments before responding.

"What do you know about Nok Woo Lee?"

"Not much."

"Are you friendly?"

"I've spoken to the man."

"When?"

"The last time I was in San Francisco."

"And what was the occasion?"

Clint shrugged.

"I just needed some help on something."

"And he supplied it?"

"He . . . entertained me. Is he still around?"

"Oh, he's around."

"Then maybe he'd help."

"Maybe he'd help you," McGowan said. "He's not about to help me, or any other policeman."

McGowan sat staring at the coffeepot.

"Would you like some coffee?"

"Hmm? Oh, no, thanks. I had breakfast."

"Then maybe you'd better get going to Chinatown."

"Yeah," McGowan said glumly, "maybe I'd better." He stood up, made as if to leave, then turned back.

"Will you be staying around San Francisco?"

"I suppose I will."

"Maybe you'll get a chance to talk to Lee."

Clint stared at the inspector, then said, "Maybe I will. You never know."

McGowan nodded, turned, and left.

Clint was halfway finished with his second pot of coffee when Allan Marks walked in.

Why wasn't he surprised?

TEN

"I waited until McGowan left," Marks said.

"Have a seat."

Marks sat down, leaned back, and stared at Clint.

"You didn't kill those people just to make sure I'd stay in town, did you?" Clint asked.

Marks snapped his fingers and said, "I didn't think of that. Will you be staying around?"

"I think so."

"Why?"

Clint shrugged and said, "I guess I want to find out if it's the same guy."

"Somebody's got to *catch* him before you find that out," Marks said. "You think McGowan's gonna do that?"

"No."

"Who, then?"

Clint didn't answer.

"Are you gonna try to catch him, Mr. Adams?"

"That would make a good story, wouldn't it?"

"It sure would."

"Well, don't print it."

Marks sat forward.

"Does that mean you are?"

"No comment."

"Come on, Clint," Marks said, "this is just me and you. Did I print anything today that we talked about yesterday?"

"We didn't talk about much yesterday."

"Come on . . ."

"What do you want me to say, Marks?"

"That you're going after this crazy man! Jesus, somebody has to, somebody who cares!"

Clint looked across the table at the newspaperman, who seemed to sincerely believe what he was saying.

"Maybe you should say that in your newspaper," Clint said. "Maybe that would force the police to put someone on the case who was going to give it his best effort."

Marks sat back and said, "You might be right. Maybe I should do that. But I still think you're the man to get the job done."

"I'm sorry to disappoint you."

Marks frowned.

"Maybe you could get in touch with Bat Masterson?"

"What for?" Clint was surprised by the suggestion.

"Maybe he'd want another chance to catch this killer, don't you think?"

That hadn't occurred to Clint. The last he'd heard of Bat he was in Denver. If he saw a newspaper about the murders here in San Francisco, would he think it was the same killer? Would he come to San Francisco?

"I don't know where Bat is," he said.

"Well, wherever he is, maybe he'll see the newspaper accounts."

"Maybe." Suddenly he thought of something. "You said you read the old Dodge City newspapers?"

"That's right. We have an extensive morgue in the *Call* building."

"What about checking other newspapers between then and now?" Clint suggested. "Maybe you can find some other towns where this happened."

"That's an idea," Marks said. "That's a damned good idea."

Clint thought so, too. He also thought that it was a good idea for Marks to follow up, not him. He didn't relish wading through years of newspapers.

"Well," Marks said, "I can't do any more here."

He stood up but took his time leaving, as if he thought Clint might have something more to say. When nothing more was forthcoming, he finally left the table and walked out.

Clint replayed both conversations in his head, and two things stuck with him. From the conversation with Marks, the thought that Bat Masterson might become interested in what was going on and come to San Francisco.

From his talk with the policeman, Inspector McGowan, he was thinking about Nok Woo Lee. Lee had helped him find that Japanese sword the last time he was in San Francisco, but there had been a fee involved. Men like Lee never did anything just out of the kindness of their hearts. If he was going to go to Lee for help, he would have to be prepared to pay a fee—and the fee would not always be money. Still, nobody knew Chinatown like Nok Woo Lee.

ELEVEN

Clint walked down Ross Alley. He was surprised that the murder had taken place so close to Nok Woo Lee's place. He was also surprised that a prostitute would be plying her trade that close.

Lee's place was all the way at the end of Ross Alley. Clint knocked on the door and at about eye level a small cutout opened and a pair of eyes appeared. As soon as they saw Clint, they widened in surprise, then crinkled in amusement.

The door opened and Nok Woo Lee appeared. The first time Clint had seen him he'd been surprised. He'd been expecting a Chinese, and Nok Woo Lee turned out to be white. He'd been born on a ship and left behind in China by his parents. A Chinese family had raised him, and when he was old enough he got on a ship and came to the United States.

"Clint Adams."

"Hello, Lee."

"It's been what . . . a year?"

"Less than that."

"How's your big Japanese friend?"

He was referring to Toshiro Matsu, a Japanese warlord Clint had helped recover his emperor's sword. He had not seen Matsu since the man returned to Japan.

"I don't know," he said. "We don't exchange letters."

"Come in, come in," Lee said, backing away so Clint could enter.

Lee was about thirty, still slender and just under six feet, still looking more like a schoolteacher than what he was. He was dressed Western style, shirt and trousers, rather than the "coolie" pajamas he'd been wearing last time.

"I'm adopting the dress of my homeland," Lee said, spreading his arms as if modeling the clothes.

"They fit you well."

"Please, precede me."

Clint walked ahead of Lee until they reached his living quarters. The man might have adopted Western style dress, but there was still no furniture, just pillows strewn about.

"To what do I owe this pleasure?" Lee asked.

"There was a murder in Ross Alley last night."

"Ah, yes," Lee said. "A Chinese girl."

"And a white male."

"Yes," Lee said, nodding, "a white man. A friend of yours?"

"No. I didn't know him."

"Then why . . ."

"The first man," Clint said, "Jason Birch. He was killed in a den I suspect you probably own."

"I do not admit to that."

"He was my friend."

"And why are you here now?"

"To ask you for your help."

"Aren't the police handling this matter?" Lee asked.

Clint nodded. "An Inspector McGowan."

"Ah, now I see," Lee said.

"You know McGowan?"

"Very well. Once he was a good policeman."

"And now?"

Lee smiled. "And now he isn't."

"That's what I thought."

"What do you want me to do?"

"Tell me what you know."

"And why should I?"

"Because I'm asking."

Lee considered that, then shook his head.

"I will help you, but not for that reason."

"A fee, then?"

"No."

"Then why?"

"Because the killer had the audacity to commit his murders just feet from my door," Lee said. "Also, the girl worked for me."

Now it was Clint's turn to say, "Ah. Does that mean you would help the police if they came to you?"

Lee laughed.

"No," he said, "it does not. Besides, they would never come to me—but you have."

"Yes."

"What do you know, Clint Adams?"

"I don't know much," Clint said. "I suspect a lot."

"And what do you suspect?"

Clint briefly explained to Lee about Dodge City and the murders committed there.

"This is interesting," Lee said when Clint was done.

"Do you have any information, Lee?"

The man shook his head.

"Alas, I do not."

"Have you heard of this before?"

"I have heard of murder many times before," Lee said, "and I have heard of murders in Chinatown, but I have never heard of a series of murders committed by one man."

"What can be done?" Clint asked.

"Questions will be asked," Lee said, "inquiries made, and I will look into this other matter."

"The Dodge City murders? How?"

Lee smiled.

"My . . . reach goes beyond San Francisco Chinatown, my dear friend."

Clint wondered when they had become friends.

"I will do some research and get back to you," Lee said. "Where are you staying?"

Clint told him.

"You could do better."

"I'm comfortable."

"I could get you a room at any—"

"I'm fine, Lee," Clint said.

"Very well, then," Lee said. "When I have some information I shall send for you."

"Fine."

Lee walked Clint to the door.

"Be careful in Ross Alley," Lee said. "I would not want you to become a victim."

"It's not dark," Clint said, "and I'm alert. The killer prefers to catch men when their . . . minds are otherwise occupied."

"That does appear to be true."

"I'll thank you in advance for your efforts, Lee," Clint said.

"Chinatown may be a threat to many people," Lee said, "but it is my home, my safe haven, and it has been invaded. I cannot tolerate that. I will defend my home, just as any other man would."

"I understand and appreciate that, Lee."

Lee smiled.

"I knew you would."

TWELVE

Clint returned to the hotel, wondering what more there was for him to do until he heard from Lee. When he arrived the desk clerk quickly called him over. He was a young man, impressed with the fact that the famous Gunsmith was staying at the hotel. Now he seemed even more impressed than ever.

"You got a telegram while you were out, Mr. Adams," he said excitedly.

"And?"

The young man looked around, then leaned forward and said, "It's from Bat Masterson!"

"Can I have it?" Clint asked in the same low tone.

"Oh, of course." The young clerk handed it over.

"Thank you."

Clint moved a few feet away and read the telegram. It was from Bat, as the clerk had said, and it had come from Denver. Bat said he'd be arriving tomorrow night

47

on the train, and that he wanted Clint to meet him at the station.

It was possible that Bat had read about the first murder in the newspaper, but he could not have heard about the second one yet. Also, how did he know that Clint was in San Francisco, and what hotel he was staying at?

Why did he suddenly have the feeling that he and Bat had strings attached to them, and someone was pulling them?

Clint was at the station when Bat arrived. He watched his friend step down to the platform, carrying only a small carpetbag. Bat looked around, saw Clint coming toward him, and moved forward to meet him. They shook hands and looked at each other solemnly.

"What's going on?" Bat asked.

"I wish I knew."

"I got a telegram telling me about the murders," Bat said. "I don't know who sent it."

"What did it say?"

"That there were some murders in Chinatown that I might be interested in. It didn't say who was murdered."

"One was a Chinese prostitute and a white man I didn't know."

"And the other?"

"You know Jason Birch."

Bat looked at him quickly.

"I do—or, I guess, I did."

They got a cab from the station to Clint's hotel, and on the way Clint told him how Birch had been killed.

"Just like Dodge City," Bat said.

"Yes."

"What about the other one?"

Clint told him about the man and the whore killed in a doorway.

"It doesn't fit exactly," Bat said, "but I guess it's close enough. Do you think it's the same killer?"

"Well, I didn't . . ."

"But you've changed your mind?"

"Well," Clint said, "who sent you that telegram?"

"You think it was him?"

"Who else?"

Bat thought about that for a while.

"I don't like being manipulated," he said finally.

"Neither do I," Clint said, "but this does bring an interesting point to mind."

"Like what?"

"Somebody knew where you and I were," he said.

"Only some of my friends knew where I was," Bat said.

"And mine," Clint said. "Also, if the same killer is at work here as was in Dodge City—"

"I think I see where you're heading," Bat said, "In Dodge I kept thinking that the killer had to be a drifter, a stranger."

"Right."

Bat looked at Clint.

"You're saying that the killer is someone we know."

"That's what I'm suggesting."

"Like who?"

"That's the question, isn't it?" Clint asked. "Who?"

THIRTEEN

When they arrived at the hotel they registered Bat and had his bag taken to the room, then went into the hotel bar. They each got a beer then found a back table. This bar had no gaming tables, and so no matter what time of day or night you went in, you were able to find a table. Most people were over in Portsmouth Square after dark.

"You know what this means, don't you?" Bat asked. "We have to suspect everyone who was in Dodge with us then."

"Except each other."

"Right," Bat said, "and Ed."

Bat's brother Ed had been killed in Dodge City a couple of months before the murders took place.

"And Jim."

Jim was Bat's other brother, who was also a lawman in Dodge at the time.

"And Wyatt," Clint said.

"Right, Wyatt."

Clint went over the chronology in his mind. Ed was killed in April of that year, Jim arrived in June, and Wyatt soon after—and then the murders took place during the last portion of the year.

"Who does that leave?" Bat asked.

Clint looked across the table at him and said, "That leaves an awful lot of people. . . ."

FOURTEEN

Dodge City
Six Years Earlier...

That year Dodge City had become Queen of the Cow Towns and was on its way to becoming Mistress of the Gamblers. Charlie Bassett had taken over as marshal from the deceased Ed Masterson. Jim Masterson was a deputy marshal, while Wyatt Earp was an assistant marshal. Bat Masterson was sheriff.

Clint Adams was just visiting.

The first murder took place a week after Clint arrived. A man had his throat cut while in Chinatown looking for a prostitute.

"If you weren't my friend," Bat said one night, "I'd suspect you."

"Well, then, I'm glad I'm your friend," Clint said.

"Are there any other strangers in town you could suspect?"

"This is Dodge City," Bat said. "It's full of strangers."

They were in the Crystal Palace, which was full of strangers. As Clint looked around, though, there were a lot of familiar faces, as well.

Luke Short was playing poker across the room, at the same table with Dave Mather. Also gambling that night were Cockeyed Frank Loving, Dick Clark, and Ben Thompson's brother, Billy. Ben would appear in town later that month.

Not gambling but standing at the bar were Colonel Charles Goodnight and Eddie Foy, the vaudeville performer who had opened at the Comique during July.

Clint looked across the table at Bat and saw that his friend was looking at the crowd, as well.

"Any one of these people could be the killer," Bat said. "I just have to figure out which one."

"How do you propose to figure it out?"

"I don't know," Bat said. "I'm not a detective, Clint. Why doesn't Charlie Bassett catch the guy?"

"Charlie's the marshal," Clint said. "As sheriff this falls to you."

"Yeah, yeah," Bat said, turning his beer mug around and around. "You know, maybe it was a random thing."

"Maybe."

"Maybe it won't happen again."

"That could be."

"Maybe," Bat said, "the killer will just leave town."

"Let's hope so."

The killer did not leave town. A week later he struck again, killing a man while he was lying in an opium crib. Once again, the victim's throat had been cut. In addition, a Chinaman who was working in the opium den was killed the same way.

That night Clint and Bat sat at a table in the Lady Gay, trying to develop a strategy for catching the killer.

"So what are you going to do?" Clint asked.

"My job, I guess," Bat said.

"Bring in Bassett, and Jim. Talk to Wyatt."

"I can do that," Bat said, "but in the end the problem is mine."

"Wyatt will help."

"I know he will, Clint."

Clint had met Bat Masterson and Wyatt Earp at the same time, when they were all young buffalo hunters. Over the years his friendship with Bat had deepened more than it had with Wyatt, but they were all still friends.

"Who the hell is this guy?" Bat asked, frustrated. "If he wants to kill people, why doesn't he just use a gun, like the rest of us?"

"Obviously, he's a coward," Clint said, "somebody who has to sneak up on people and kill them without confronting them."

For the better part of a half hour Clint and Bat tried to build some sort of profile of the kind of man who would commit these kinds of murders. They decided that he was frightened, he had low self-esteem, and he probably had never been with a woman, which frustrated him.

"That's why he's killing men who are seeking their pleasures in Chinatown," Bat said.

"Listen to us," Clint said. "Do we even know what we're talking about?"

"I think we do," Bat said. "I think I have an idea

who to look for now. Thanks for talking it over with me, Clint.''

''Sure, Bat,'' Clint said, even though he wasn't quite as sure as his friend was that they had hit on something.

After Bat left, Clint decided to play some poker instead of brooding about the killings, and over the course of the next several hours he gave the matter no thought.

FIFTEEN

Clint managed not to think about the murders all night by bringing a girl back to his room with him. Her name was Lila and she worked at the Lady Gay. Normally, when she spent the night with a man she charged him for it, but she and Clint had been making eye contact for most of the evening, and when Clint invited her to go back to his room with him, she accepted.

"I don't mean as a customer," he'd said. "I mean, I don't pay for sex."

"Well," she'd said, "you're just going to have to show me why you don't have to pay for it."

He showed her three or four times during the night.

In the morning he woke to find her hands on him. She was rubbing his chest, and then slid her hand down over his belly.

"What are you doing, woman?" he asked.

She smiled and he noticed that she had a crooked

tooth he could only see when she smiled widely. She had an interesting face rather than a pretty one, and the crooked tooth added to the attraction. He found himself responding to her touch very quickly.

"I'm waking you up," she said.

"You have an interesting way of doing it."

"Wait," she said, sliding one thigh over him, "it gets even more interesting."

As she mounted him, he could smell her and feel how wet she was. She rubbed her wet pussy on him, purring as she did so, and then she raised her hips, reached between them, and inserted him into her. She sat up on him, using all her weight to drive him deeply inside her. She was a slender girl, but she had large breasts and large brown nipples. As she rode him he cupped her breasts to his face and sucked the nipples, sometimes taking both of them into his mouth at the same time. When he did this she'd go crazy and start bouncing up and down on him harder. Finally he just gripped her hips and watched as her breasts bounced around, listened to the sound their flesh made as their crotches came together, and then watched in fascination the look that came over her face when her pleasure overcame her. Her eyes widened, as if she had seen something that surprised or frightened her, and her face became flushed, and then she squeezed her eyes shut and bit her lip and rode him for all she was worth. . . .

Lila left his room first, saying she had to get back to her own room to get some sleep so she would look halfway rested when she reported for work. Clint apologized for keeping her awake. She kissed him good-bye soundly and said he could keep her awake like that anytime he wanted.

An hour later Clint came down for breakfast and was

on his first pot of coffee when Wyatt Earp walked into the dining room and joined him.

"Poor Bat," Wyatt said.

"Because of the murders," Clint asked, "or is there something I don't know?"

"The mayor and the town council are talking to him right now," Wyatt said. "They want something done about this killer."

"He's doing what he can," Clint said. "He's not a detective."

"None of us are," Wyatt said, meaning both Mastersons, Bat and Jim, as well as Charlie Bassett. "If they want a detective maybe they should hire one."

The waiter came over and took Wyatt's order for breakfast.

"Just bring me what he's having," Wyatt said.

"So what can we do?" Clint asked.

"I don't know," Wyatt said. "Ask questions, I guess. Look around. Be a presence. Maybe we can keep it from happening again."

Clint recalled that was just about what he and Bat had said after the first killing.

"I guess we'll all just have to do our best."

"You want to wear a badge?"

"No."

"I didn't think so, but I knew you'd help, anyway."

"Why wouldn't I?" Clint asked. "Bat's my friend."

"Mine, too, but I'm glad I'm not in his shoes."

Reluctantly, Clint said, "Yeah, me, too."

While they were eating breakfast Jim Masterson walked in and joined them. Two years younger than his brother Bat, Jim was Dodge City's deputy marshal.

When the waiter came over, Jim said, "I'll have what they're having."

Clint and Wyatt filled Jim in on what they'd decided,

and he allowed as he couldn't think of anything else to do.

"Maybe they'll fire Bat," he said.

"What good would that do?" Wyatt asked.

"Well, if that happened I'd quit, and then me and Bat could leave. We could say to hell with Dodge City then. Let somebody else try to catch the killer."

"You think Bat would stop looking then?" Clint asked.

"No," Jim said, "but it was just a thought. Naw, Bat's too insulted now. He wants the killer bad."

"So do we all," Wyatt said.

Clint thought that they all wanted him for Bat's sake and that was fine, but he knew that nobody wanted him as much as Bat did.

SIXTEEN

For the next week all of Bat's friends tried to be a threatening presence, in the saloons, on the streets. Wyatt and Clint often walked the streets together in the evening, including Chinatown. Jim Masterson sometimes spelled one of them, walking with the other.

Charlie Bassett and some of his other assistant marshals did the same.

Bat started questioning all of the strangers in town, or anyone he thought had come to town since just before the murders. The town council had given him a tepid vote of confidence, but the mayor told him he was getting pressure to replace him.

"I asked him who he was going to replace me with and the son of a bitch didn't have an answer. You know?" Bat asked Clint. "Because there is no one to replace me with. If he puts Jim or Wyatt into the job, he'll have the same problem."

So Bat still had his job for a while, and for a week nothing happened.

And then something did.

Clint and Jim Masterson were walking toward Chinatown when they saw someone running toward them. It was a white man, and he was moving quickly. When he saw the badge on Jim's shirt, he stopped short.

"You better come quick."

"Where?" Jim asked.

"Chinatown."

"Lead on."

They followed the man until he led them into the dark, tented streets of Chinatown to a place Clint knew was a Chinese brothel.

"Inside," the man said.

"Where?"

"One of the cribs, in the back."

When they entered they were met by an older Chinese woman who was wringing her hands. Clint assumed she was the madam. She was chattering away in Chinese, but none of the three men paid her any mind.

"Back here," the man said.

They entered the crib and saw a man lying on a pallet, his chest covered with blood. The blood had come from a gaping wound in his throat.

Behind them a couple of girls entered, wearing filmy robes and lots of face paint.

"Who was with him?" Jim asked.

They stared at him blankly.

"No speakee English?" Jim asked.

Again, blank stares.

"I think we should burn this place to the ground," Clint said.

"No!" one of the girls protested.

Clint grinned at Jim and said, "She understood that."

Jim looked at the girl and asked, "Who was with him?"

"Soon Yee."

"And where is she?"

The girl indicated the girl next to her.

"She say he alive when she leave," the first girl said.

"What's your name?"

"Ona Zee."

"That your real name?" Clint asked.

She shook her head. It really didn't matter, though.

Clint looked around and said, "Where's the fella?"

"What fella?" Jim asked.

"The one who showed us here."

"Never mind him," Jim said. "We got to get Bat here. Who goes, you or me?"

"You're in authority here," Clint said. "I'll go."

"Okay," Jim said, "hurry back."

Clint left, thinking about the man who'd brought them there and wondering where he'd gone, but the man was forgotten in the wake of the murder.

There was one more murder after that, then the killings stopped abruptly. The mayor and the town council congratulated Bat, who took no credit.

"The man just stopped," he said to Clint later. "What did I—or any of us—have to do with that?"

The town didn't care how the killings stopped, just that they did—especially the people in Chinatown. The killings had been a threat to their businesses.

Clint left Dodge City a short time later and didn't ever think of those killings again until San Francisco, six years later.

SEVENTEEN

San Francisco
Six Years Later . . .

Bat stared across the table at Clint.

"Somebody we know," he said, shaking his head. "There were a lot of people in Dodge that year, Clint."

"How many during the time of the murders, Bat?" Clint asked.

"A lot," Bat said. "I can't really accept that it was one of us."

"Us," Clint said. "Bat, 'us' was you, me, Jim, Wyatt, and Charlie Bassett. I think we can rule us out."

"Why get me here, though?" Bat asked. "And you?"

"I was already here," Clint said. "But he deliberately sent you a telegram. That means he wants to try you again. He wants to see if you can catch him this time."

"Here?" Bat asked helplessly. "I couldn't catch him

in Dodge City. This is San Francisco, ten times—twenty times—the size of Dodge. How could I catch him here?''

''Well, for one thing, we know more.''

''Like what?''

''Like he's not a stranger to us.''

''Maybe he was back in Dodge,'' Bat offered.

''No,'' Clint said, ''I think he knew us in Dodge.''

''Why do you say that?''

Clint shrugged.

''Just a feeling I have. This is somebody who knows us—you, specifically—and wants to play again, after six years.''

''So you think he's just been laying low until now?''

''I don't know. There's a newspaperman here who's doing some research into that.''

''He should probably look at Leadville.''

It was the birth of mining boomtowns like Leadville, Colorado, that signaled the end for towns like Dodge City. In fact, many of the merchants, gamblers, and saloon owners who had lived and worked Dodge City for two years actually left Dodge *for* Leadville.

''You know, that's not a bad thought,'' Clint said. ''Luke Short spent a lot of time in Leadville. Maybe he'd know something.''

''Luke's in New York.''

''Oh? What for?''

''What else?'' Bat said. ''Poker.''

''Do you know where he's staying?''

''Where he always stays when he's in New York,'' Bat said. ''I'll get a telegram off to him and ask him if he knows of these kinds of killings taking place in Leadville.''

''Okay, good,'' Clint said. ''Meanwhile, I had a talk with someone here who might be able to help us.''

"Who was that?"

Clint explained Nok Woo Lee to Bat, who listened intently.

"Sounds like an interesting man."

"He is."

"The question is, will he be helpful?"

"I guess we'll just have to wait and see."

Bat finished his beer and pushed the empty mug away.

"You probably want to get some rest after your trip, Bat," Clint said.

"I am kind of beat."

"We can talk more about this in the morning," Clint said. "I have some more to tell you."

"If you told me now," Bat said, "you'd probably just have to repeat it again."

They both stood up and walked out to the lobby.

"You want to meet down here in the morning for breakfast?" Clint asked.

"Sure. How's nine a.m. sound?"

"Fine."

"See you then."

The two friends shook hands and Bat went up to his room. Clint left his hotel and walked to Portsmouth Square.

Across the street the killer watched as Clint Adams left the hotel. He correctly assumed that Bat had gone up to bed. As Adams walked toward Portsmouth Square the killer was content to remain in his doorway. All the players were in place now. Tomorrow the game would begin in earnest.

When Clint Adams was out of sight, he stepped out and headed back to his own hotel, a fleabag on the Barbary Coast.

EIGHTEEN

Clint stopped at the Alhambra that night.

"Hey, Mr. Adams."

Clint had just stopped at the bar when he heard his name. He turned and saw one of the men he and Jason Birch had played poker with the night Birch was killed.

"Wade Tyler, remember?" the man said. "Played poker with you and Birch."

"I remember."

Tyler came and stood next to him at the bar.

"Haven't seen much of you since that night," the man said. "You promised us a chance at gettin' our money back, if I remember correctly."

"Yes, I did," Clint said, "but a lot's happened since then."

"Yeah, you mean Birch gettin' himself killed," Tyler said. "That was too bad. He took a lot of my money that night. I sure would have liked a chance to get it back."

Clint turned and faced Tyler.

"The man got his throat cut and all you're worried about is your money?"

"Hey," Tyler said, sensing he'd done something wrong, "I didn't mean—"

"Get away from me, Tyler," Clint said. "I won't drink with you."

"Hey, all I meant was—"

"I know what you meant," Clint said. "Go away!"

Tyler backed off a few steps, then turned and hurriedly walked away.

"Give me a beer, please," Clint said to the bartender.

At the other end of the floor, Dean Williams watched Wade Tyler come walking toward him.

"Well?"

"He, uh, ain't gonna play."

"Why not?" Williams asked. "Hey, him and that other fella took a lot of our money. Now that other fella's dead and Adams ain't gonna give us a chance?"

Tyler sat down.

"He's real sensitive about Birch bein' killed."

"That ain't fair!" Williams complained. "We didn't have nothin' to do with that. He should give us a chance to get our money back from him, at least."

Tyler picked up the beer he'd been working on before he went over to Clint and said, "Why don't you walk on over there and tell him that, Dean?"

Instead, Williams picked up his beer also and glowered into it.

"I didn't think so," Tyler said.

Williams sat quietly, fuming.

"You know what, Dean?"

"What?"

"I think we should get our money back, one way or another," Tyler said. "What do you think?"

Dean Williams smiled.

Clint nursed a beer at the bar for a while. He didn't know what he was doing there. He didn't feel like gambling and didn't feel like talking to anyone—but he didn't feel like going to bed either.

He decided he needed some air. He left the Alhambra with the intention of walking around Portsmouth Square, maybe stopping into some of the other saloons and clubs just for something to do. It didn't take long, though, before he realized he was being followed.

He crossed the street and ducked into the first alley he came to. It was dark but he could hear footsteps coming quickly, as if whoever was following him was afraid he'd lost him. Suddenly, a man came into view and Clint stepped out of the alley, grabbed him from behind, and dragged him back into the alley with him.

"Hey—" the man protested.

He was smaller and lighter than Clint, so holding him was not that big a problem.

"Stop struggling," Clint said, "and stay quiet or I'll break your arm."

Abruptly, the man stopped.

"Stand still."

Clint released the man and searched him. He relieved him of a gun that was in a shoulder rig, tucked it into his own gun belt, and then backed away from the man.

"Okay, talk," Clint said. "Why are you following me?"

"I'm just following orders."

"Whose orders?"

"Inspector McGowan."

"You're a policeman?"

The man nodded.

"Show me your badge."

The man took out his badge and showed it to him.

"Why didn't you say something?"

"Y-you said you'd break my arm."

Clint handed the man back his gun.

"You're not very good at following someone, are you?"

"I guess not," the man said sheepishly.

"Let's step out into the light."

They left the alley and Clint saw that the policeman was very young, in his early twenties.

"What's your name?"

"Arthur."

"Is that your first or last name?"

"First . . . my name's Arthur Pine."

"Why is Inspector McGowan having you follow me?" Clint asked.

"I don't know," Pine said. "He told me to do it and I'm doing it."

"He didn't tell you why?"

"No, sir."

"Or what to look for?"

"No, sir."

"What did he tell you?"

"Just to follow you and to remember what I saw you do, and who I saw you with."

"And do you intend to continue following me now that we've spoken?"

"Well . . . yes, sir. Those are my orders."

"Well, then, for your information I'm just taking a walk around the Square. I'll probably drop in and out of places. I'm just killing time, not doing anything in particular. All right?''

"Yes, sir."

"Don't follow too close, though," Clint said. "I might meet a woman, you know what I mean?"

The young man looked puzzled and said, "No, sir."

"That's okay," Clint said, "you don't have to."

Clint wondered if McGowan had deliberately chosen someone incompetent to follow him, or if he had seriously assigned the task to this young man. Was the inspector so incompetent himself that he failed to recognize it in others?

And this was the man who was going to catch the Chinatown killer?

NINETEEN

Clint made the rounds of some of the saloons and gambling houses. Each time he went into one he checked to see if Pine was still with him, and he was. The young policeman would stand at the end of the bar, order a beer, and nurse it. By the time they would leave a saloon most of the beer was still in the mug. The man was trying not to get drunk, Clint surmised.

Finally, Clint decided he'd had enough and would turn in for the night. He started back to his hotel, with Pine trailing along behind him.

He was crossing Montgomery Street to his hotel when he heard his name, and then a shot. He dropped quickly to one knee, drawing his gun. He saw a man step from the shadows near the hotel door, and the glint of moonlight off a gun. He had only a split second to react and decided it was better to be alive and wrong than dead and right. He fired and heard the man grunt as the slug struck him in the chest. He staggered forward, dropped his gun, and fell facedown into the street.

Clint rushed to the fallen man and turned him over. It was Tyler, the man who had spoken to him at the Alhambra, the man he and Birch had played poker with.

He heard footsteps behind him and turned quickly. He saw Arthur Pine standing there with his gun out.

"Mine's dead, too," Pine said.

"Who was it?"

"I don't know," Pine said. "He was across the street, and as you turned he stepped out to fire. He was going to shoot you in the back!"

Clint shivered. He'd been convinced for a long time—ever since Bill Hickok had been shot in the back by a coward—that he was going to die the same way.

"So I shot him," Pine said.

"Let's take a look," Clint said.

They both holstered their guns and walked to the first man. Clint turned him over and recognized him.

"Know him?" Pine asked.

"Not by name," Clint said. "I played poker with both these boys. I guess they're bad losers."

He turned and looked at Pine.

"Looks like I owe you," he said. "Thanks."

"Just doing my job," Pine said.

"Well, you better keep doing it and arrange to have these boys collected."

"Right."

"You know what happened so you won't be needing me. I'm going to turn in."

"Okay."

"Are you going to be following me tomorrow, Pine?" Clint asked.

"I don't know," Pine said. "I guess I'll get my orders in the morning."

"Well," Clint said, "if you are going to be following me, I'll be coming down at nine a.m. to have breakfast with Bat Masterson. Why don't you join us?"

Pine looked overwhelmed by the invitation. He puffed out his chest and said, "It would be an honor, sir."

"You saved my life tonight, Arthur," Clint said. "Stop calling me sir, and call me Clint."

"Yes, s—I mean, sure, Clint."

"Good night, Arthur."

"Good night."

Clint crossed the street and entered his hotel. When he got to his room Bat Masterson was standing in the hall, bare-chested and barefoot, wearing Levi's and holding his gun. He'd gotten a room right down the hall from Clint's.

"What the hell is going on?" he demanded.

"I'll tell you in the morning," Clint said. "Nothing to do with the killer, just a couple of sore losers."

"We've all run into them in our lives, haven't we?" Bat asked.

"I guess we have," Clint said. "Good night, Bat."

"Night, Clint."

TWENTY

Clint came down to the hotel lobby first to wait for Bat. When he got down there he saw Arthur Pine waiting, along with Inspector McGowan.

"Good morning," Clint said to them both.

"I understand you invited my young officer to breakfast," McGowan said.

"That's right," Clint said. "I owe him at least that for what he did last night."

Pine looked embarrassed.

"Mr. Adams," McGowan said, "I don't like the idea of you trying to bribe my man."

"Bribe him?" Clint asked. "With breakfast?"

"With whatever," McGowan said. "He was only doing his job last night."

"I think he was doing more than that."

"How so?"

"He said his job was to watch me and remember what

he saw," Clint said. "Well, he could have watched me be killed, but he decided to step in and lend a hand."

"That *is* his job," McGowan said. "He will not be having breakfast with you."

"Too bad."

McGowan turned to Pine.

"You can go to work now, Officer Pine."

"Yes, sir."

With that Pine turned and left the hotel.

"Is there some reason you're still here, Inspector?" Clint asked. "You're not expecting me to buy *you* breakfast, are you?"

"Of course not," McGowan said. "I understand Bat Masterson arrived last night."

"Now how would you know that?"

"It's my job to know things," McGowan said.

"I thought it was your job to catch a killer."

"I don't need you to tell me what my job is, Mr. Adams."

"Well, somebody has to, if you think that keeping a watch on me and Bat is going to accomplish anything."

"What is Masterson doing here?"

"Why don't you ask him?" Clint replied. "He'll be down any minute."

"If you and Bat Masterson have any idea of interfering with a police investigation—"

"We don't."

"That's good."

"We just think the killer should be caught," Clint added. "We don't particularly care who catches him . . . do you?"

"Never mind what I think," McGowan said. "Just remember what I told you."

"Are you going to be having someone watching me today, Inspector?"

"Just remember what I said," McGowan repeated. With that he turned and left.

"Pompous, useless ass," Clint said aloud.

"Who is?"

He turned to see Bat approaching him.

"Come into breakfast and I'll tell you who is," he said.

"You also owe me an explanation about last night," Bat said. "The shooting woke me up."

"I'll tell you all about it," Clint said, "over steak and eggs. . . ."

Clint told Bat about finding Arthur Pine on his tail, and then how Pine had saved his life.

"I guess you were pretty lucky last night," Bat said. "This Pine could have been a bad shot. And what about the two men?"

"Birch and I beat them in poker the night he was killed. They've been looking for a chance to win their money back ever since."

"So they finally decided just to take it back?"

"I guess that was their thinking."

"This is all very distracting," Bat said. "What about the pompous ass?"

Clint told Bat about Inspector McGowan and everything he'd learned and surmised about the man.

"Apparently," he finished, "he doesn't think he can catch the killer, but he doesn't want anyone else to either."

"It'll make him look bad."

"He's doing a good job all by himself of making himself look bad. He doesn't need much help with that."

"I get the feeling we're not talking about a reliable policeman here."

"Not at all."

"What about this reporter you mentioned?"

"His name is Marks, and he writes for the *Morning Call*."

"Didn't Mark Twain work for that paper some years ago?" Bat asked.

"Yes," Clint said, "about twenty years ago."

"So what kind of fella is this Marks?"

"He seems to have a certain degree of passion for what he's doing," Clint said.

"Is he as underhanded as most newspapermen?"

"I haven't seen any evidence of that, yet."

"Is he the one doing research on these kinds of killings?"

"Yes."

"Then we should tell him about Leadville."

"I was thinking of stopping up to see him today."

"I'm very interested in this other fella you mentioned, this Nok Woo Lee."

"That's understandable," Clint said. "He's an interesting guy. I'm hoping to hear from him soon. Nobody knows Chinatown like he does."

"Well, nobody knows Dodge City the way it was six years ago like we do," Bat said. "The way it was, and the people who were there. I would think we'd be able to figure this out, Clint."

Clint appeared distracted.

"Clint?"

"Hmm? Oh, sorry, Bat. I was just wondering . . ."

"Wondering what?"

"Well, if the killer sent you that telegram as an invitation," Clint said, "I wonder if he's finished."

"Who else would he, uh, invite?"

"How about Wyatt?"

"It's possible, I guess," Bat said, "but I was the sheriff of Dodge City, and you just happened to be here, anyway.''

"Coincidence," Clint said, shaking his head.

"I know how you hate coincidence, Clint, but that could be exactly what it was."

"And what if seeing me here is what got him started again?" Clint asked.

"Now you want to take the blame for his killings?" Bat asked. "Don't do that to yourself. If he was going to get started again he would have, eventually. Maybe it will be to his misfortune that he saw you and got started, if that's the case, because then he decided to invite me, and if anybody can catch him, we can . . . especially if it's someone we know."

"That's something we should go over," Clint said. "Who was there, who we can eliminate . . ."

"Well, then, let's get another pot of coffee and start going over names," Bat suggested.

TWENTY-ONE

For the better part of the next hour Clint and Bat bandied names about from Dodge City, six years earlier.

Ben Thompson was there, but while the legendary gambler and gunman was not a particular friend of Clint's, he agreed with Bat that the man was not a crazed killer.

"What about Billy?" Clint asked, referring to Ben Thompson's younger brother.

"No, not Billy," Bat said. "Billy wouldn't do anything Ben didn't tell him to do."

"Wasn't Tilghman around then?" Clint asked.

"Yeah, Bill was around. In fact, he's the law in Dodge right now."

"I didn't know that. I guess we can eliminate him, especially if he's in Dodge right now."

"I'd never suspect Bill."

As it turned out, there was a long line of men they

would each never have suspected. Each other, to start, then Bat's brother Jim, Charlie Bassett, Wyatt Earp, the aforementioned Thompson brothers, as well as Bill Tilghman. After that the list went on: Luke Short, Doc Holliday ("He was kind of crazy," Bat said, "but he did his killing with a gun."), Nat Kramer, "Doctor Neil," Cockeyed Frank Loving, Johnny Green, Ton Lane . . . these were all gamblers, they reasoned, not killers.

"If we're going to keep eliminating people," Clint finally said, "we're not going to have anyone left."

"Well, those were the gamblers who came to town," Bat said. "What about the ones who worked for the saloons?"

"Dick Clark, of course," Clint said. Clark was one of the most well-renowned faro dealers.

"We can eliminate him, he was never a killer. How about Trick Brown?"

"Trick wouldn't be caught dead in Chinatown," Clint said. "J. J. Harlan?"

" 'Off-wheeler,' " Bat said, using Harlan's nickname. "He would be powerful enough. The man's stronger than a mule, but gentle."

"And Jim Moon?" Clint asked.

"Hot-tempered," Bat said. "He'd kill in anger, at a moment's notice."

"What about Charlie Goodnight?"

"No, not Goodnight." Bat offered no reason.

"Eddie Foy?"

"He was an entertainer, not a killer."

"President Hayes?"

Bat laughed.

"President Rutherford B. Hayes," he said, "never left his railroad car after he got the first whiff of the cattle pens."

That was true, Clint remembered. Hayes had been on a tour of the West with General William T. Sherman, and had emerged from his car to hear a welcome speech from Mayor Kelley, but the aroma from the pens had driven him back inside, and he never came out again.

"That'd be interesting, though, wouldn't it?" Bat asked. "If President Hayes turned out to be the killer?"

"That would be more than interesting," Clint said.

So after an hour they were no closer to identifying someone who *could* have been the killer in Dodge City, let alone San Francisco.

"I think I better go and talk to Marks about including Leadville in his research. What are you going to do?"

"I haven't been to San Francisco in a while," Bat said. "I think I'll take a walk around the Square."

"You better be careful."

"I'm always careful, Clint," Bat said, as they stood up from their table, "you know that. But I don't think we need to fear anything from this killer. He's too much of a coward to face either one of us, and besides, if he kills us his game is over."

As they walked out, Clint opined that maybe they should be concentrating on the cowardly aspect of the killer's makeup.

"All right," Bat said, "let's both think back to Dodge City to try to figure out who the biggest cowards were."

No small task, they both thought, as they separated.

TWENTY-TWO

When Clint reached the offices of the *Morning Call* and asked for Marks, he was told that the reporter was down in the morgue. Obtaining directions, Clint made his way to the basement of the building and found Marks poring over old newspapers.

"Hey," Marks said when he saw Clint, "I didn't expect to see you down here."

"I didn't expect to be down here."

Marks sat back from the stacks of newspapers in front of him.

"Why *are* you down here?"

"Leadville."

"What?"

"Bat Masterson got here last night . . ." Clint said, and went on to explain what he and Bat had been talking about since his arrival.

"Do you think Masterson would do an interview?"

Clint glared at Marks.

"Okay, never mind," Marks said. "I'm sorry. How have you and Bat been doing, trying to come up with a name?"

"We've come up with plenty of names," Clint said, "but we keep eliminating them."

"What's this about Leadville?"

"Leadville drew a lot of people from Dodge City," Clint said. "We were wondering if there was any record of these kinds of killings in Leadville."

"Did Leadville have a Chinatown?"

"I don't know if it had something *called* Chinatown," Clint said, "but it had an Oriental population."

"Leadville . . ." Marks said. "Okay, I'll take a look."

"You might as well check some of the other mining towns, as well," Clint said. "Gunnison, Ouray, Silverton, Aspen—"

"I'll check them all out, Clint," Marks said. "I think the newspaper in Leadville was called the *Union*."

"How would you know that?" Clint asked. "I've been there and I don't know it."

"I've made a study of western newspapers," Marks said. "I'm a student of them."

Clint stared at the young man, impressed in spite of himself.

"You know," Clint said, "if you're not careful you might end up changing my opinion of newspaper people."

"I hope so," Marks said. "At least, maybe this newspaperman."

"Maybe."

"Uh, if I do that, would you give me an interview?"

"Now you're pushing it," Clint said.

"Hey," Marks said, "I had to give it a try."

• • •

Bat was walking around Portsmouth Square, taking in the sights, wishing he was there simply to gamble, when he realized he was being followed. Remembering what Clint had told him about being followed, he hoped that his tail was also a policeman, but he couldn't just accept that. He quickened his pace and started to look for a place to confront the man.

Finally, he turned a corner and quickly stepped into a doorway. As the man passed him, he stepped out and pressed his gun into his back.

"Oh!" the man said, and raised his hands.

"Why are you following me?"

"Would it do any good to tell you I wasn't?"

"No."

"Can I reach into my pocket?"

"Slowly."

The man did so and came out with a badge.

"You're not Pine, are you?"

Arthur Pine nodded, his shoulders slumped.

"Clint was right," Bat said, putting his gun away, "you're not very good at this, are you?"

"I guess not."

Bat looked across the street and saw a small saloon.

"How would you like me to buy you a drink?"

Pine turned around and frowned.

"Why?"

"I want to talk to you."

"About what?"

Bat clapped the young man on the shoulder and said, "I'll tell you over a beer."

"I don't know," Pine said, "I could get into a lot of trouble—"

"With who?"

"Inspector McGowan."

"You know what?" Bat said. "We won't tell Inspector McGowan."

Pine was still hesitant.

"I don't know," he said, "you buying me a drink, that could be a bribe—"

"A what? Mr. Pine, who is filling your head with such nonsense?"

Pine frowned again and said, "Inspector McGowan."

"I'm starting to think that this Inspector McGowan is a very bad influence on you."

"He's my boss," Pine said. "He's teaching me how to be a detective."

"He's teaching you how to be a bad detective, I think," Bat said. "Come on, Pine, what the inspector doesn't know won't hurt him. It's time for a drink."

TWENTY-THREE

When Clint got back to the hotel Bat was sitting in the lobby on a sofa, reading one of the free newspapers. As Clint got closer, he saw that it was the *Call*.

"Finished your walk?" Clint asked.

"I had an interesting one," Bat said, setting the newspaper aside. "I ran into a friend of yours."

"Oh? Who?"

"Arthur Pine."

Clint laughed.

"I wondered where he was," he said. "McGowan had him following you?"

"He sure did."

"What did you do to him, Bat?"

"I bought him a drink."

"Why?"

"I wanted to talk to him."

Clint sat next to Bat on the sofa.

"About what?"

"About working with us."

"Pine?" Clint asked. "He struck me as kind of straightlaced."

"I found that out," Bat said. "He said me buying him a drink would be looked on by Inspector McGowan as a bribe."

"Jesus," Clint said, shaking his head, "he's young."

"Too young for me to get through to," Bat said. "When we left he hadn't touched the beer I bought him, and he insisted that he could not go against Inspector McGowan. Oh, this'll interest you. He also said that McGowan is teaching him how to be a detective."

"Yeah," Clint said, "a bad detective."

"That's what I said."

"And what did he say?"

"He didn't think it was funny. How did you do with the newspaperman?"

"Allan Marks," Clint said, reminding him. "He even knew the name of the Leadville newspaper. He's going to research the Colorado boomtowns and get back to us."

"You sound impressed by him."

"Against my better judgment, I am. He doesn't seem like the usual newspaperman."

"I've always found them to be all the same," Bat said. "I'll be interested in meeting this one."

They sat quietly for a moment in the hotel lobby, watching people come and go.

"What the hell do we do now?" Bat asked.

"He's got us waiting," Clint said, "waiting for him to strike again."

"I feel helpless," Bat said, "and I don't like it."

"I know what you mean."

"What about your Chinaman who's not a China-man?" Bat asked. "Lee?"

"Nok Woo Lee," Clint said. "I think we just have to wait on him, too. He doesn't respond well to pressure."

"Waiting," Bat said, "I hate waiting."

"Let's get something to eat."

"Late lunch?" Bat asked.

"Early dinner," Clint said.

"Where?"

"Somewhere on the Square."

Bat slapped the newspaper down on the sofa, intending to leave it there.

"Let's go."

They rose together and walked out the front door, stopping just outside.

"We're thinking the same thing," Bat said.

"I know," Clint said. "Where is he?"

"Is he across the street, watching us from some doorway or window?"

"We can't let him see us waiting," Clint said. "We've got to act normally."

"Eat," Bat said, "drink . . . and gamble."

"That's what we'll do, then," Clint said, "starting with the eating part."

"And let him watch," Bat said. "To hell with him."

TWENTY-FOUR

Clint ate his dinner thoughtfully, wondering if he and Bat weren't being a little silly, thinking that they were being watched by a killer. Maybe it was even sillier to believe that the man had lured Bat to San Francisco to play games with them both.

"What are you thinking?" Bat asked.

"What makes you think I'm thinking anything?"

"I can smell the burning from here," Bat said. "Come on."

Clint told Bat his thoughts, and Bat shook his head.

"You're thinking we're conceited, thinking we might be the reason this crazy man is killing—wait a minute. *I* don't think I'm the reason, do you?"

"Not the reason, exactly," Clint said. "I mean, he's crazy, that's the reason he's doing it, but what if he was . . . I don't know . . . retired, or something, and seeing me gave him the hunger again."

"If you think that way," Bat said, "then it's your fault I'm here."

"You're right," Clint said, "I am being silly. I can't start taking blame for you being here."

"No," Bat said, "I had a lot to do with that, myself, so why don't you just forget the rest of it, too. Let this fella take the blame for what he's doing."

"You're right."

"See?" Bat said. "When I ask you what you're thinking you have to tell me, so I can set you right."

"I'll keep that in mind," Clint said. "More coffee?"

They not only had more coffee, but each got a piece of peach pie. Clint was pouring coffee for Bat when there was some commotion at the front door of the restaurant. They both looked that way and saw two of the waiters trying to force a Chinaman out the door. The Chinaman was, in turn, trying to get someone's attention.

"He wants you," Bat said.

"That's what I thought," Clint said, putting the pot down and rising.

He made his way to the door and pushed the two waiters away.

"Leave him alone."

"Sir, he's not allowed—"

"I'll take care of it," Clint told the man. He held his hand up, palm out, and made a pushing motion. "Just get away."

The two waiters backed off, and Clint noticed that most of the other diners were staring.

"Just go back to your meals, folks," he said. "There's nothing to see here."

He turned to the Chinaman and saw that he was a boy, barely eighteen or nineteen.

"Are you looking for me?"

"You are Gunsmith?"

"Yes."

"I lookee for you."

"Let's go outside."

The boy nodded and they both stepped outside.

"What can I do for you?"

"Nok Woo Lee sent me," the boy said in perfect English. "He wants to see you."

"You can speak English."

"Very well."

"What was that 'lookee' stuff?"

The boy smiled.

"I just give them what they expect."

"What's your name?"

"Wing."

"Just Wing?"

Again the boy smiled.

"It is enough."

"Well, Wing, when does Lee want to see me?"

"As soon as possible."

"Okay," Clint said. "You tell Lee I'll be along later this evening, and I'm bringing a friend."

Wing frowned.

"Lee said just you."

"You tell Lee I'm bringing Bat Masterson," Clint said. "He won't have a problem with that."

"Very well," Wing said with a slight bow. "I will tell him."

"Thank you," Clint said.

"Thank you," Wing said, "for not letting them throw me out."

"That's all right, Wing."

Wing bowed again, then turned and went off at a trot.

•   •   •

"What was that about?" Bat asked when Clint returned to the table.

Clint sat down, then looked around to see who was watching them. Several people turned their heads away quickly.

"Do you still want to meet Nok Woo Lee?" Clint asked Bat.

Bat looked surprised.

"Sure."

"Well, finish up your pie and you'll get your chance. He wants to see me tonight."

"With me along?"

"Trust me," Clint said. "He'll be thrilled."

TWENTY-FIVE

Clint led Bat down Ross Alley toward Lee's, pausing to show him where the man and whore were killed. When they reached Lee's door he knocked, and the little cutout door opened, then closed quickly.

The door opened and Lee stepped out, grinning broadly.

"You brought him," the man said. "When Wing said you would I didn't believe him."

When Clint told Bat that Lee would be thrilled to meet him he was kidding, but apparently that was exactly the case.

"Nok Woo Lee," Clint said, making the introductions, "this is Bat Masterson. Bat, Nok Woo Lee."

"It's a pleasure to meet you," Lee said, shaking Bat's hand.

"Likewise."

"I've heard so much about you," Lee said. "Please, come in."

Clint and Bat entered, and Lee closed the door, then led them to his living quarters.

"I wish we had some time to talk," Lee said to Bat. "Perhaps you would join me for dinner some evening while you are here?"

"I can't say at the moment," Bat replied. "Clint and I do have some business to complete this week."

"Ah, yes," Lee said, "business."

"I hope you asked me to come here because you have some information," Clint said.

"Not much information, I'm afraid," Lee said, "but perhaps a morsel."

"What kind of morsel?"

"One of the other girls told me that Tina—she is the girl who was killed—had been soliciting men from the Barbary Coast."

"So?"

"My girls have strict instructions to stay away from the Barbary Coast," Lee said.

"You don't like the clientele there?" Bat asked.

"I don't want my girls being stolen and sent overseas on some freighter," Lee explained.

"I thought white women were stolen," Bat said. "That's why they call it white slavery."

"There is a market for any kind of woman overseas, Bat . . . may I call you Bat?"

"Of course."

"So you think the killer spotted your girl and her customer on the Coast?"

"It's possible," Lee said. "Tina's the only girl who disobeyed my orders, and now she's dead. As I understand it, Clint, you are a firm disbeliever in coincidence."

Bat snorted and said, "You've got that right. He hates them."

"Well, then," Lee said, "I suspect you had better widen your search area to include the Barbary Coast."

"I expect you're right, Lee."

"I'll keep my ears open for anything further," Lee promised.

"We appreciate it," Clint said.

Lee looked at Bat.

"Perhaps you'll repay my assistance by sitting and talking with me awhile before you leave San Francisco?"

Bat looked at Clint, who simply shrugged.

"Perhaps," Bat said.

"Excellent."

"Would that be your entire fee for your help, Lee?" Clint asked.

"I thought I explained that before, Clint," Lee said. "No fee. After all, you are searching for the killer of one of my girls. No, I do not want Bat to feel . . . obligated to me. I only want him to come by if he wants to."

"I can't make any promises," Bat said, "but I'll try."

"That's good enough for me," Lee said. "I'll see you both out."

At the door Lee paused and then said, "There's one more thing."

"What's that?"

"You should beware a man named Three-fingered Mike Jolly."

"Jolly?" Bat repeated.

"Never heard of him," Clint said.

"Well, he is what you would call the top vice lord on the Barbary Coast, at the moment."

"At the moment?" Bat asked.

Lee looked at him.

"It changes hands fairly often," he explained. "They kill each other off and take over until somebody kills another one and takes over, and so on."

"That doesn't happen here, in Chinatown?" Clint asked.

Lee smiled and said, "Not as often. I'm just warning you to watch your step, but considering the reputation you each carry, perhaps I should be warning him, instead."

"We'll keep Three-fingered Mike in mind, Lee," Clint said. "Thanks."

"So tell me something," Bat said to Clint as they left Ross Alley.

"Like what?"

"Does he, uh, like girls?"

"Does he like— Oh, I see." Clint looked at Bat with a big smile on his face. "Don't tell me you're suspicious of his invitation."

Bat looked uncomfortable.

"Haven't you ever heard of men who, uh, prefer other men?"

"Well, sure I have," Clint said, "but what did Lee do to make you think he might, uh, prefer you?"

"Well, has he ever invited you?"

"Uh, well, no, he hasn't."

"See," Bat said, "and you're much prettier than I am."

Clint laughed.

"Pretty's not a word I'd use for either one of us," he said.

"Well, then, I guess I just appealed to him."

"I think maybe he's just impressed with your reputation, Bat," Clint said.

"And he isn't impressed by yours?"

"I guess not."

"Hmmm . . ."

"It's your decision," Clint said. "What could it hurt to go and talk to the man for a little while before you leave town?"

"Let's do what we have to do first," Bat said, "and then I'll decide."

"Fine," Clint said. "It's late, but the Barbary Coast should just be getting started about now. Are you game for a look tonight?"

"Why not?" Bat asked. "I haven't seen the Coast for some time . . . and we can watch each other's backs so *we* don't end up on a freighter."

TWENTY-SIX

The Barbary Coast was Portsmouth Square stripped of its finery, its class, its law—the Coast was stripped of just about everything but vice. You could find a woman in the Square, and on the Coast, but on the Coast it was considered a vice. The same could be said for gambling.

The Barbary Coast catered to a rough trade of men, most of them off the ships that came into the harbor. Many of those men had been at sea for weeks, perhaps months, and were looking to cut loose. The law on the Barbary Coast made itself scarce, and so men like Three-fingered Mike Jolly, and Glass-eyed Tommy Tuttle before him, often proclaimed themselves the law.

Clint and Bat had both drank and gambled on the Barbary Coast before. Individually they'd each think twice about going back, although if they had a reason they would. Together, however, they were reasonably certain they could handle anything that came along. They had done so in the past, many times, against heavy odds.

They stopped first in a saloon called the Bucket of Blood. The place was about half full, as there was no gambling available, just beer and whiskey. About half of the patrons were clad in Western garb, and the others were dressed as seamen.

"A Chinese prostitute would sure stand out in here," Bat said as they approached the bar.

"I'll say."

"What are we looking for anyway?" Bat asked.

"Maybe we'll know it when we find it."

The bartender glared at them as they reached the bar.

"Two beers," Clint said.

The man drew the beers and set the mugs down on the bar top hard, so that some of the beer spilled.

"Four bits," he said, as if daring them to argue the price.

Clint paid and said, "Thanks."

"Pleasant sort," Bat said.

He turned his back to the bar to survey the room, while Clint remained with his elbows on the bar, watching the bartender. They had watched each other's backs so often it had become second nature over the years.

"I don't see anything," Bat said, "and the beer's warm."

"Maybe we're not here to see anything, after all," Clint said.

"What's that mean?"

"Maybe we're here to be seen."

"By the killer, you mean?"

Clint nodded.

"Well, if he's someone we know," Bat said, "that means if he sees us, we'll see him."

"Maybe," Clint said. "He could be in a doorway, or on a rooftop."

"Or nice and snug in a hotel room with a girl," Bat said.

Bat looked at his beer, shuddered, and put it down on the bar.

"I think we should try someplace else," he said, "to see or be seen."

"Why not?"

Clint put his warm beer down, too.

"Hey!"

Clint and Bat stopped as they were turning away from the bar. They looked back and saw the bartender glaring at them again. He was a big, beefy man with wiry gray and black hairs on his massive forearms. Right now he had his arms folded so that his hands were both out of sight.

"You talking to us?" Clint asked.

"Whatsamatta?" the barman asked belligerently. "You don't like our beer?"

"As a matter of fact," Bat said, "we don't."

"Bat . . ." Clint said warningly.

"Hey, boys," the bartender shouted, "these fancy Dans don't like our beer."

Chairs scraped the floor as several tables discharged their occupants.

"Jesus," Clint said, "we've only been here five minutes. . . ."

The men from the tables started moving toward Clint and Bat. Some of them were seamen, probably armed with knives or dirks, while others were more traditionally dressed and armed—with guns, although none of them were drawn, yet.

"I'm not about to collect any bruises," Bat said.

"Well, I don't feel like killing anybody," Clint said. "Maybe we should just drink the beer."

"No," Bat said, "it's warm."

"Well, then I guess we'd better just leave."

"You ain't leavin'," the barman said, "not when you insulted my beer."

"Friend," Clint said, "do you want somebody to get hurt over some warm beer?"

"Yeah," he said, "you. Get 'em, boys."

"What do you suggest?" Bat asked. "Running?"

"I don't feel like running."

"Then toes?" Bat said, drawing his gun.

"Toes," Clint agreed, drawing his.

TWENTY-SEVEN

When the first two men lost a toe each, the others all stopped their rush short. The two men with bloody feet sat down on the floor and clutched them.

"You're gonna be sorry you did that," the bartender said.

"Not today, we're not," Clint said.

"Anybody steps outside after we leave," Bat said, "we'll shoot a little higher."

"Knees are a lot easier target," Clint said.

Bat and he backed up until they were outside, then they turned and walked away. They both ejected the empty shells from their guns and reloaded.

"You're slipping," Bat said. "I took off a little toe, you took off a big one."

"I wasn't feeling charitable," Clint said.

"Where to now?"

"Another saloon?"

"Word is going to get around, you know."

"I know," Clint said. "Do you want to go back to the hotel?"

"No," Bat said after a moment, "we're here, we might as well just continue on."

"I wonder if any of those men work for Three-fingered Mike Jolly," Clint said.

"If they do I guess we'll find out about it soon enough, won't we?"

Back in the Bucket of Blood the bartender came around the bar and looked down at the two wounded men. Then he looked at the others standing around.

"Pick them up and get them out of here," he said.

"Sure, boss," one of them said.

The bartender watched as the two injured men were picked up and carried out, directed by the first man, whose name was Neil.

"What should we do with them, boss?" Neil asked.

"Just get them to a doctor, then pay them off," Three-fingered Mike Jolly said. "They're fired."

"Okay, boss. Uh, what about those two fellas?"

"Do you know who those two fellas were?" Jolly asked.

"Uh, no . . ."

"Clint Adams and Bat Masterson."

Neil's eyes widened.

"If you knew who they were, why'd you send us after them?" he asked.

Jolly laughed. His right hand was hanging down by his side, his left was hidden from view behind his back. It was his left hand that only had three fingers. He did an amazing job of hiding it from view, even when he was tending bar.

"I wanted to see them in action."

"Well, you did that."

"Toes," Jolly said, shaking his head.

He took off his bartender's apron, went around the bar to retrieve his hat and jacket.

"I'm done for the night, Neil," he said. "Get somebody else to tend bar."

"Okay, boss. Uh, what are you gonna be doing?"

"I'm going for a walk."

"Want somebody to go with you?"

"No, Neil, I don't," Jolly said. "If I did, I would have said so."

"Right, boss."

"I tell you what," Mike Jolly said, "why don't you tend bar for a while, Neil. It helps keep you in touch with people."

"Me?"

"Yeah, Neil," Jolly said, "you."

Jolly went outside and stopped just in front of the place. He looked both ways, wondering which way Clint Adams and Bat Masterson might have gone. He didn't see them at all, but he figured they'd be going further into the Barbary Coast than away from it. They didn't strike him as the types to walk away easily.

He turned left and started walking.

TWENTY-EIGHT

Clint and Bat managed to stop in two more saloons without incident. They also managed to get at least one cold beer. They were drinking that cold one at a back table in a place called Dead Man's Drink.

"It figures the beer would be cold at a place called Dead Man's Drink," Bat said.

"Company," Clint said.

Bat looked at the door and saw the bartender from the Bucket of Blood standing just inside.

"Guess he got off work and came here for a drink," Bat said.

"Or trouble," Clint said. "He's headed this way."

"He doesn't have a gun," Bat observed.

"Let's hear what he has to say."

The man reached the table and stared down at the two of them.

"You've got to be Masterson," he said, pointing at Bat, "and that makes you Adams."

"Now that we know who we are," Clint said, "who are you—besides the bartender at the Bucket of Blood?"

"I'm also the owner of the Bucket of Blood," he said.

"And?"

"And the owner of this place, and half the places you've been in tonight."

Bat and Clint exchanged a glance.

"I guess that would make you . . ." Bat started.

The man took his left hand out from behind his back and they saw that he had only three fingers on it.

". . . Three-fingered Mike Jolly," Clint said.

"That's right," Jolly said. "Mind if I sit?"

"Sure," Clint said, "it's your place, isn't it?"

Jolly sat in the chair between them and put both of his hands on the table. The three-fingered hand drew the eyes of Bat and Clint.

"Don't ask," Jolly said.

"Wasn't going to," Clint said. "What can we do for you, Mr. Jolly?"

"What are you doing on the Barbary Coast?" Jolly asked. "You've been in and out of a dozen saloons, and all you did was buy one beer in each." Jolly pointed to the beers in front of them and said, "These are the first beers you're finishing."

"These are the first cold ones we've found," Bat said.

"Who sent you?"

"Nobody sent us," Clint said.

"What are you lookin' for?" Jolly asked.

"A killer," Clint said.

"What?"

"He said, 'a killer,' " Bat repeated.

Jolly looked at one, and then the other.

"You want to hire a killer?" he asked. "Men with your reps?"

"We don't want to hire one," Bat said, "we want to find one."

"Anyone in particular?" Jolly asked.

"Yes," Clint said, "the one who has killed two men and a woman in Chinatown."

"Chinatown? Well, then, what the fuck are ya doin' on the Barbary Coast? Why don't you go to Chinatown and find your killer?"

"We've been to Chinatown," Clint said. "Somebody told us that the dead girl was working the Coast."

"A Chinee girl workin' the Coast?" Jolly asked. "Who sent you here? That bastard Lee? Knock Wood Lee?"

"Knock Wood?" Bat said. "I thought his name was Nok Woo, or something."

"Around here he's Knock Wood," Jolly said. "What did he tell you about me?"

"He warned us to be careful," Clint said. "He said you were deadly."

"You don't look deadly," Bat said. "You aren't even armed."

"I'm armed."

"Got a hide-out gun?" Bat asked. "In your boot, maybe?"

"Look around you," Jolly said.

Clint and Bat did so. The saloon was almost full.

"All I have to do is say the word and half of these men will draw their guns and kill you."

"One word?" Clint asked.

"It's like that all over the Barbary Coast," Jolly said. "Hell, the whole Coast is my weapon."

"If the Coast is so completely yours," Clint said, "then you can help us."

"I might be able to," Jolly said, "but why should I?"

"If you don't," Clint said, "this maniac is going to keep on killing."

"And tell me again why I should care?"

"When he gets tired of killing people in Chinatown," Clint said, "he might decide to come here, to the Coast."

"That would be his biggest mistake."

"Why?"

"He couldn't go ten feet without me knowin' about it," Jolly said.

"And you have enough men to take care of him."

"That's right."

"Like your men took care of us at the Bucket of Blood?" Bat asked. "Last I remember, two of them were missing toes."

"Like I said," Jolly said, "one word from me and you're both dead."

"Maybe," Clint said.

"But you'd be dead first," Bat said.

"Count on it," Clint said.

Under the table both Clint and Bat cocked the hammers back on their guns. Jolly jerked a bit, and sat up straight in his chair.

Clint and Bat stood up, both pointing their guns at Mike Jolly.

"Think it over," Clint said. "We'd be real grateful for your help, Mike."

They backed toward the door, everyone's attention on them now. The tension in the room was thick, like heat waves in the desert.

"Easy," Mike Jolly told his men, holding up his hands so nobody would do anything stupid. "Let them go."

"See you again, Mike," Clint said.

"You won't be happy if you do," Jolly replied.

Clint and Bat watched each other's backs until they were out the door, and then away from the Barbary Coast completely.

TWENTY-NINE

"Well, that accomplished a lot," Bat said as they got back to their hotel.

"We got a cold beer."

"The Barbary Coast sure has gone downhill," Bat said. "I remember at least being able to get a cold beer."

"What did you think of Jolly?"

"What's to think?" Bat asked. "He seems to have the Coast under his thumb—until somebody kills him."

Bat looked over at the hotel bar and saw that it was still open.

"Feel like a decent beer?"

"Sure, why not?" Clint asked. "I'm a little too wound up to go to sleep, anyway."

"Yeah," Bat said as they walked toward the bar, "shooting off somebody's toe always does that to a fella."

When they entered the saloon, the first person they

saw was Arthur Pine, sitting alone at a table. His hang-dog look brightened when he saw them come in. He got up and rushed toward them.

"What are you doing here?" Clint asked.

"I was supposed to be following you."

"Both of us?"

"Well, yes, if you were together, but you, Mr. Adams, specifically."

"And?"

Looking chagrined, he said, "And I lost you."

"Come on, Pine," Bat said, "we'll buy you a beer."

"Uh, I don't think—"

"Don't give me any of that bribe stuff, Pine," Bat said. "Go and sit down with Clint. I'll bring the beer."

Pine followed Clint to an empty table in the back of the room. Bat joined them moments later, putting three beers down on the table.

Pine looked at his beer and then at Clint and Bat.

"I don't think I can—"

"Pine, Pine," Bat said patiently, "be a man, drink the damn beer."

Pine looked stung, then picked up the beer mug, took a sip, and set it down.

"Attaboy," Bat said.

"Arthur," Clint said.

"Yes, sir?"

"What do you know about Mike Jolly?"

"Three-fingered Mike Jolly? He owns all of the vice on the Barbary Coast, and has for the past year. Tommy Tuttle owned it before him, but rumor has it Mike Jolly killed Tuttle."

"Killed him," Clint asked, "or had him killed?"

"No, we believe he killed Tuttle himself."

"What about Nok Woo Lee?" Bat asked. "What do you know about him?"

Pine shrugged.

"He's Jolly's counterpart in Chinatown," the young policeman said, "except that he's been in power a lot longer. Why are you asking about these two men?"

"We saw them both today," Bat said.

"Both of them?" Pine asked incredulously.

"That's right."

"I've *never* seen Lee," Pine said, sounding awed that they had, "and I've only seen Jolly once. Why were you seeing them?"

"Are *you* asking?" Clint asked. "Or is this for Inspector McGowan?"

"Oh, uh, I was just curious. . . ."

"We were hoping they could tell us something about this killer," Clint said.

"And did they?"

"Well, no . . ."

"Lee recommended that we look on the Barbary Coast for our killer," Bat said.

"Why the Coast?"

"Apparently the whore who was killed was working the Coast as well as Chinatown."

"Lee's girls aren't supposed to do that," Pine said.

"So we understand," Bat said.

"Maybe he killed her."

Clint and Bat both looked at Pine.

"What?" Bat said.

"Maybe Lee killed her for working the Coast," Pine suggested again.

"You think he killed his own girl?" Clint said. "And a customer?"

"It, uh, was just an idea," Pine said.

"I don't think Lee would kill a potential customer," Clint said. "It would be bad for business."

"That's giving him a lot of credit for intelligence," Pine said.

Clint looked at Pine.

"You don't think Lee is intelligent?"

"Well . . . the inspector doesn't think so."

"Inspector *McGowan* doesn't think so?" Clint asked incredulously.

Pine looked away and said, "He's not so bad . . . really."

"Open your eyes, lad," Bat said. "It looks to me like the only thing he's doing to try and catch this killer is to have you follow us."

Pine looked at them, his eyes almost pleading, and said, "He must be doing something else!"

"If he is," Clint said, "I'd sure like to know about it."

"You don't mean you want me to spy on the inspector," Pine said.

"Not spy, exactly," Bat said, "just sort of keep an eye on."

"We'd just like to know that he is doing something else, Arthur," Clint said. "I'm sure you want to know that, too."

"Well . . . yes—I mean, I'm sure he is . . . he must be."

"Why don't you find out for yourself, Pine," Bat said.

"And if you do that, you can let us know, too," Clint said. "We'd like to know for sure that the inspector is doing his best."

Pine thought a moment, one hand wrapped around the beer, and then a determined look came over his face.

"I'll do it!" he said.

"Good man," Bat said.

"You'll be doing it for your own peace of mind, Arthur," Clint said.

Pine looked at each man in turn, then looked at his beer. An even more determined look came over him and he raised the mug to his mouth and drained it. He brought the mug down to the table with a bang.

"Get yourself a good night's sleep, Arthur," Clint said. "You can get started in the morning."

"I'll start in the morning," the young man said, as if it was his own idea.

"Good night, Arthur," Bat said.

Pine marched out of the bar with a determined step.

Clint and Bat exchanged a look and then Clint said, "We may have just gotten that boy in a whole lot of trouble."

THIRTY

The consensus of opinion between Clint and Bat was that they might have gotten Arthur Pine in some trouble, but at least he'd be out of their hair for a while.

"We're just lucky he didn't follow us to the Barbary Coast," Clint said.

"Maybe *he's* lucky he didn't follow us," Bat said. "He might have gotten himself hurt."

The consensus was formed on their way to bed, and again agreed on at breakfast. The only thing they couldn't agree on in the morning was what they should be doing that day.

"I'm not in favor of trolling the Barbary Coast again," Bat said.

"Not even in the daytime?"

"Not with Mike Jolly upset with us," Bat said. "We might end up having to kill him."

"But look on the bright side."

115

"And what's that?"

"If we kill him, we'll end up owning the Barbary Coast."

Bat gave that all the thought it deserved and said, "I don't want to own the Barbary Coast. That's all the more reason we shouldn't go back there."

"Chinatown, then?"

Bat made a face.

"What are we going to find out there that Nok Woo Lee can't find out?"

"Nothing," Clint said. "You're right."

They asked for and received another pot of coffee, and Clint did the honors of pouring.

"What does that leave us, then?" Bat asked.

Clint shrugged.

"Another trip down memory lane?"

"Back to Dodge, you mean?"

Clint nodded.

"We went through that already," Bat said. "We dredged up the names of everyone we knew in Dodge during that time, and eliminated them one by one."

"Maybe we shouldn't have eliminated all of them," Clint suggested.

"Like who?" Bat asked. "Who should we put back on the list as a suspect? Tilghman?"

"No."

"Charlie Bassett?"

"No."

"Wyatt?"

"No!"

Bat spread his hands helplessly.

"You tell me, then."

"Maybe," Clint said, "we should just go over that last day."

"Why?"

"Because he never killed again after that," Clint said. "Maybe something happened that day that stopped him."

"Like what?"

"I don't know," Clint said. "Why don't you tell me about that day, Bat? From start to finish."

"Well," Bat said, rubbing his jaw, "I was frustrated as hell . . ."

THIRTY-ONE

Dodge City
Six Years Earlier . . .

Bat woke that morning with a raging headache. It was either from drinking too much last night, or from the tension caused by the man the newspaper was calling the Chinatown Assassin. Why they chose the word "assassin" he didn't know. It probably sounded more exotic than calling him the Chinatown Killer.

When he got to his office he put on a pot of coffee, making it strong because he knew Clint would be along shortly. The one constant about his friend since the days when they met while hunting buffalo was his liking for strong, black coffee.

Bat had just seated himself behind his desk when the door opened and Clint walked in.

"Coffee's made," Bat said, lifting his boots up onto the desk.

"You look like hell," Clint said, pouring himself a cup and then sitting opposite his friend.

"I feel like hell."

"This killer is really getting to you, huh?"

"I'm just sitting around waiting for him to strike again," Bat said. "I feel damn helpless."

There were copies of the *Dodge City Times* and the *Ford County Globe* on Bat's desk. Both newspapers were writing a story a day about the murders.

"Why do you read those?" Clint asked. "Just throw them away."

Bat touched the papers and said, "They're calling for my head, because this is my responsibility."

"Maybe you should call in some help, Bat," Clint said.

"Like who?"

"Like a real detective. I could send a telegram to Talbot Roper in Denver."

Bat scowled. He didn't like to admit that this was beyond him.

"By the time he got here and we filled him in—"

"If I know Roper," Clint said, "he's following this story in the newspapers."

"That's another thing," Bat said. "This story is probably being picked up by other newspapers across the country."

"Your ego is bruised."

"Damn right it is," Bat said, surprising Clint. He hadn't expected his friend to admit it so readily. "Wouldn't yours be?"

"I suppose so."

"No, maybe it wouldn't," Bat said. "You're more resistant to that sort of thing than I am."

"Am I?"

"You're not like everyone else, Clint," Bat said. "You don't really buy into your own reputation."

"And you do?"

"Sometimes," Bat said, "yeah, sometimes I think, 'Hey, I'm Bat Masterson,' and sometimes I don't know who Bat Masterson is."

At that moment the door opened and Wyatt Earp stepped in.

"Speaking of reputations . . ." Bat said.

"I smelled coffee," Wyatt said.

"Have some."

He walked over to the coffeepot and poured himself a cup.

"What are we discussing," he asked, "as if I didn't know?"

"Reputations," Bat said.

"Egos," Clint said.

Wyatt sat down and said, "Lord knows I've got my fair share of both of those. Funny, I thought you'd be discussing the murders."

"We are," Clint said.

"That's how we got on the subject of egos."

"Oh," Wyatt said, eyeing the newspapers on Bat's desk.

"You've read these?"

"I have," Wyatt said. "They're not being fair to you, Bat."

"Don't I know it," Bat said.

"They're scared," Clint said.

"Why?" Wyatt asked. "All people have to do is stay out of Chinatown."

"You know," Bat said, "the editor of the *Times* was doing a whole bunch of articles about that a few months ago. Neither of you were here, then."

"Who's he?" Wyatt asked.

"Some young Easterner hired by the Shinn brothers to run it."

"What's his name?" Clint asked.

Bat shrugged.

"I guess I don't know."

"Well, maybe we should find out," Clint said.

"What *was* his name?" Clint asked, bringing Bat back to the present.

Bat rubbed his jaw and said, "I can't remember."

"One of us went and talked to him, didn't we?"

"I think so," Bat said. "Who was it? You?"

"Not me. I thought it was you."

"It was Wyatt," Bat said. "I remember now. He talked to him and said he was a stiff-collared Easterner who was trying to make a name for himself as another Horace Greeley."

"And did he, I wonder?" Clint asked.

"I don't know," Bat said. "I guess if we found out his name, we'd know."

"We'll have to do that," Clint said. "Why don't you finish telling me about that day."

"You were there, Clint," Bat said. "You know what happened that day. There was another murder, we were called to the scene of it, and we almost caught the bastard. . . ."

THIRTY-TWO

Dodge City
Six Years Earlier . . .

Clint and Bat were in the Crystal Palace when the man came running in. He stopped just inside the door, spotted them, and hurried over.

"You better come quick, Sheriff."

"Where?"

"Over the Dead Line," the man said, which is where the murders had been taking place, in the Chinese section. "Somebody's gettin' killed."

"What do you mean—"

"Come quick!" the man said, and ran out.

Bat and Clint both got up and followed him out.

"Who was that?" Bat asked.

"I don't know," Clint said, "but he looks like the same fella as last time."

"Where'd he go?"

They looked both ways but could see no one.

"Come on," Bat said, "we better get over the Dead Line."

It was raining as they ran through the muddy streets of Dodge City.

"Hey!" they heard somebody yell, and a man came splashing up to them. It was Wyatt Earp. "What's going on?"

"Follow us!" Bat shouted. "The killer may have struck again."

"Chinatown?" Wyatt asked.

"Where else?" Clint said.

The three men ran the length of the town until they crossed the Dead Line and reached the Chinese section. They stopped beneath a tent, and the only sound they heard was the water striking the top of it.

"Well, what's going on?" Wyatt asked.

"I don't know," Bat said.

"Bat," Clint said, "neither of us knew that fella who came into the saloon."

"I was thinking that, too."

"What fella?" Wyatt asked.

"He came running in and said somebody was being killed in Chinatown," Clint said.

They all looked at each other.

"Maybe he meant somebody was *gonna* get killed," Wyatt offered.

"It's him," Bat said, slapping his thigh. "It was him. He's playin' games."

"Well," Clint said, "if that's what he's doing, then he's got to be here someplace. Let's split up and find him."

"Hopefully before he does kill someone," Bat said.

"If we do that," Wyatt asked, "how will we recognize him?"

"Let's just find somebody," Clint said.

They split up, all with their guns in hand. Clint went to one side of the street, Wyatt to the other. Bat went into the midst of the tents where the whores and opium lords plied their trade.

Since one of the murders took place in an opium den, he went directly there.

"No dead, no dead," the Chinaman who was running the place said.

Okay, Bat thought, there's nobody dead in there.

He went over to the whorehouse where a man had been killed, but the Chinese madam there insisted there were no dead men.

Bat and Wyatt reunited with Clint with water dripping off their hats.

"Nothin'," Wyatt said.

"What the hell is going on?" Clint wondered aloud.

The three men stood there, feeling like puppets whose strings had been cut.

"He got us here for some reason," Bat said. "What is it?"

Suddenly, there was a long, drawn-out scream, obviously from a woman.

"What direction?" Wyatt asked.

"Here," Bat said, pointing.

"There," Clint said, pointing.

"Okay," Bat said without hesitation, "split up again."

And they did. Bat was thinking, *You'd think if something was hurting a woman to make her scream like that she'd scream again . . . unless she was dead.*

•   •   •

It was Bat who finally found the screamer. She was huddled in a doorway with her arms wrapped around herself, a Chinese girl about nineteen or twenty.

"What happened?" he asked. He crouched down to her level and saw that she was covered with blood. "What happened?" he asked again.

She stared at him, her eyes wide with fright, and then pointed.

"You have to show me," he said.

She stopped pointing and wrapped her arms around herself again. He didn't allow that. He grabbed her by the shoulders and lifted her from the doorway.

"Show me," he said, pointing in the direction she had pointed. "Show me!"

Apparently she understood and started walking ahead of him. She led him to another doorway where a man was huddled, his trousers down around his ankles. Bat grabbed the man's wet hair and pulled his head up— and almost off! He released it and stepped back. His throat had been viciously cut . . . but why hadn't the woman been killed, as well?

"When?" Bat asked the girl.

She just stared at him.

"When did this happen?"

She didn't understand, but if it had happened when she screamed it was not long ago.

"Damn it!" he swore. The killer could still be around.

He left the girl where she was and started running. He wasn't sure where he was running to, but if the killer was still around he wanted to have at least a small chance of catching him.

Suddenly Clint Adams appeared ahead of him.

"What happened?" Clint asked.

"He hit again, Clint, and not long ago. He's got to be around here, somewhere."

"Let's go!" Clint said.

"No," Bat said, "go out into the street and stand watch. If he tries to get back across the Dead Line he'll have to go through you."

"I'll try to find Wyatt, too," Clint said.

They split up again and Bat started running, holding his gun, feeling foolish and outflanked again. The killer was probably watching him, laughing his crazy head off.

Without warning somebody stepped out in front of him from an alley and they collided. Bat went sprawling into the muddy street along with the other man, but he managed to hold on to his gun.

Was this the killer?

"Hold it right there!"

"Sheriff, Sheriff, don't shoot! It's me!"

Bat stared at the muddy figure sitting in the street a few feet from him. All he could see was white teeth and the whites of the man's eyes.

"It's you?"

"Yes."

"Who are you?"

"I'm . . ."

THIRTY-THREE

San Francisco
Six Years Later . . .

"So who was it?" Clint asked.

Bat frowned, looking across his desk at Clint, back in the present.

"He said he was the editor of the newspaper, the *Dodge City Times*."

"Okay," Clint said, "so we're back to the question of his name."

"I think he said his name was . . . I can't remember."

"Aw, Bat . . ."

"I can't remember the man's name!" Bat said defensively.

"Take it easy," Clint said. "If I remember correctly, he did turn out to be the editor of the newspaper. You told me he said the same guy that came into the saloon to get you and me also came to his office to get him."

"You know," Bat said, "I remember him now. I suspected him after that, even though I couldn't get that Chinese gal to identify him.''

"And the killings stopped after that," Clint said. "You know, I find something interesting."

"Like what?" Bat asked.

"Well, that last murder was almost identical to the most recent one here, except here he also killed the Chinese whore.''

"So he either made a mistake back then," Bat said, "or he's more thorough now.''

Clint frowned.

"I don't remember ever meeting the editor of the *Times*," Clint said.

"And I can't remember the son of a bitch's name," Bat said. "I must be getting old.''

He took a swig of his coffee and grimaced.

"So what did this little trip to the past accomplish?" Bat asked. "Except to remind me how helpless I felt back then. How foolish I felt, running around in the rain that last night.''

"We've managed to come up with two suspects," Clint said.

"You mean the editor," Bat said, "and that fella who came into the Crystal Palace that night.''

"Wasn't he the same fellow who came and got Jim and me that other time?''

"And then he disappeared," Bat said, "both times.''

"He gets my vote," Clint said. "He's the one who was playing games. He showed himself to both of us, and neither of us can remember what he looked like.''

"What about the newspaper editor?" Bat asked.

"Maybe he'd remember the other man, since he also went and got him at the office of the *Times*.''

"We could ask him," Bat said, "if I could remember his goddamn name.''

"Maybe Allan Marks can help us with that," Clint said. "After all, he's doing research into those newspapers."

"Well fine," Bat said, pushing back his chair, "let's go and ask him."

They started to leave when they saw Inspector McGowan enter the dining room with three uniformed policemen. They came directly over to Clint and Bat.

"Clint Adams," McGowan said, "Bat Masterson, you are both to come with us."

"What for?" Clint asked.

"Questioning."

"Are we under arrest?" Bat asked.

"Not at the moment," the policeman said, "but you can be if you want to."

"What's this about, McGowan?" Clint asked. He wondered if the inspector had found out what they'd talked to Arthur Pine about the night before and was angry about it. Had Pine gotten into trouble already?

"We'll talk about that when we get to my office," McGowan said. "Will you come peacefully?"

Clint and Bat both looked at the men McGowan had brought with him. They looked young, and earnest, and both men knew they'd have no trouble with them if they decided they didn't want to go quietly.

"We'll come peacefully, Inspector," Clint said. "We want to find out what this is all about."

"As if we didn't know," Bat muttered.

"What?" McGowan asked.

"I said let's go," Bat said. "Clint and I have other things to do today."

THIRTY-FOUR

Clint and Bat were taken to the police station in a police cab. Inspector McGowan sat in the enclosed back with them with one of his men while the other two men rode up top, one of them driving. Throughout the trip McGowan kept his eyes averted from them, and never spoke to them. That was fine with Clint. The less he had to talk to the inspector the better he liked it.

At the police station it was one of the uniformed men who told them to get out and then took them to an office, where he left them sitting alone. Clint knew it was McGowan's office.

"Do you think young Pine got in trouble?" Bat asked.

"Look how inept he was at following us," Clint said. "Draw your own conclusion."

"I just hope we didn't get him fired," Bat said.

At that moment the door opened and Inspector McGowan came in. He didn't speak to them, simply walked to his desk and sat down.

"Is this where we find out what we're doing here?" Clint asked.

"Or are you going to ignore us some more?" Bat asked.

"I wish I could," McGowan said, "but you two are hard to ignore."

"What did we do?" Clint asked.

"You've been to Chinatown," McGowan said, "and you were involved in a shooting on the Barbary Coast."

"A shooting," Bat said.

"Did someone complain?" Clint asked.

"You know very well that Three-fingered Mike Jolly is not going to complain to the police."

"Ah, is that who we shot?"

McGowan frowned and said, "Stop playing games, Adams. You shot two of his men . . . in the feet."

"You shot somebody in the feet?" Bat asked Clint accusingly.

"You were there, Masterson," McGowan said, "and you did it, too."

"We should be locked up," Bat said. "Imagine, shooting someone in the foot. Did they die?"

"You shot off their toes," McGowan said. "They didn't die from that."

"All their toes?" Clint asked.

"One each!" McGowan snapped. "I'm growing impatient with the two of you."

"Well, then," Clint said, "we'll leave," and they both started to get up.

"Stay where you are," McGowan said, "or I'll put you under arrest."

They sat back down, folded their hands in front of them, and stared back at him.

"You've been giving Officer Pine a hard time."

"Pine," Bat said. "Fine young man."

"Bright future," Clint said. "Don't you think?"

"He did," McGowan said, "before the two of you got ahold of him."

They did not reply to that.

"I want to know what you two think you're doing," McGowan said.

"About what?" Clint asked.

"Why were you shooting up the Barbary Coast?"

"We weren't," Clint said. "We were defending ourselves against a saloon full of Mike Jolly's men."

"You wouldn't have had to if you weren't there in the first place," McGowan said. "What were you doing there?"

Bat looked at Clint and deferred to his friend. Clint decided to stop playing word games.

"We were doing your job, Inspector."

"My job?" McGowan sat back in his chair and blinked. "What do you mean, my job?"

"Trying to find out who's killing people in Chinatown."

"And you were doing that on the Barbary Coast?"

"We got word that the dead girl was plying her trade there."

"Word from who?"

"I can't say."

"You don't have to," McGowan said. "I know you've been to see Nok Woo Lee. Are you believing what he tells you?"

"Why not?"

"He's a criminal."

"He happens to be a friend," Clint lied.

"Then you have lousy taste in friends, Adams," McGowan said.

"Hey, hey," Bat said. "I resent that."

"And what brought you to town, Mr. Masterson," McGowan asked, "and got you involved in this?"

Bat looked at Clint, whose expression told him he was on his own. Give whatever answer you want. Bat decided on the truth.

"I got a telegram."

"From who?"

"From the killer."

"What?"

"Yes," Bat said. "You see, we've met before."

"You know this killer?"

"I was after him once before," Bat said. "Six years ago I was the sheriff of Dodge City, and he was killing there."

"And did you catch him?"

"If I had," Bat said, "he wouldn't be here, doing it again."

"You're convinced he's the same killer?"

"Without a doubt."

"Why?"

"The killings are in the same style," Bat said, "and as I said, he sent me a telegram."

"Did he sign this telegram?"

"I wish he had."

"Then how do you know it's from him?"

"I know."

"You've got to give me something more than that, Mr. Masterson."

"I can't, Inspector," Bat said. "That's all I have."

"This is silly," McGowan said. "Anyone could have sent that telegram." He looked at Clint.

"Don't look at me."

"*Did* you send it?"

"I did not."

"Then someone else did."

"Right," Bat said, "the killer. To assume that someone else did it is to waste time."

"Fine," McGowan said. "What happened in Dodge City?"

"He killed five people," Bat said, "and then he stopped."

"And started just recently, here?"

"We're looking into the possibility that he's done it other places, in between Dodge and here."

"And how are you doing that?"

Clint hesitated, then said, "We've got help."

"And who is helping you besides Nok Woo Lee?" McGowan asked. "Mike Jolly?"

"Jolly?" Clint said. "He was no help at all."

"Then who?"

"I'm not at liberty to say."

"And why not?"

"Because you'll probably put pressure on him."

"Are we talking about my officer?"

"You mean Pine?" Clint asked.

"Yes, I mean Pine."

"I can honestly say that he's been no help at all either," Clint said.

"And why should he be?" McGowan asked. "He works for me."

"You should teach him how to follow somebody," Clint said. "We both spotted him."

"There's no reason why you shouldn't have seen him," McGowan said. "I wanted you to know that I was keeping an eye on you."

"Why?"

"Because I didn't want you—either one of you—interfering with my work."

"We're not interfering, Inspector," Bat said. "We're both ex-lawmen—"

"You're an ex-lawman who let this killer get away, Masterson," McGowan said, cutting Bat off. Clint saw his friend flinch.

"I suppose I am."

"Then what makes you think you can help me catch him?" McGowan asked. "Can you think of a reason I should accept your help?"

Bat firmed his jaw and said, "No, Inspector, no reason at all. In fact," he added, standing, "I'm leaving—unless you want to arrest me."

"No," McGowan said, "you can go."

"Clint?"

"I'll see you outside, Bat," Clint said. "I've got some things I want to say to the inspector."

Bat left the office and Clint looked at McGowan. What he actually wanted to do was leap across the desk at the man.

"There was no call for that," Clint said.

"For what?"

"He did his best in Dodge City," Clint went on. "He never had any training as a detective. I have to assume that you have, although I've seen no evidence of it."

"I don't have to defend—"

"Bat Masterson is more man than you ever were or will be, McGowan," Clint said, cutting the policeman off, "and you can bet your house that he'll find this killer before you do."

"I am not a betting man," McGowan said stiffly.

"That doesn't surprise me," Clint said, standing up.

"It takes a real man to put his money where his mouth is."

He left the room while McGowan was sputtering, trying to come up with an answer.

THIRTY-FIVE

"What'd you say to him?" Bat asked as Clint came outside.

"That he was a horse's ass," Clint said.

"You didn't have to do that on my account."

"What makes you think it was on your account?"

Bat smiled and slapped his friend on the back.

"What do we do next?" he asked.

"I think I ought to go and see Allan Marks."

"Without me?"

"Yep."

"And what am I supposed to do?"

"I think you should go and see Nok Woo Lee."

"And why would I want to do that?"

"Because Lee might not be doing all he could for us," Clint said.

"And if I go see him that will change?"

"He's impressed with you."

"I'm sure he is."

"No, *I'm* sure it's not what you think, Bat," Clint said. "Just go and see him, tell him some stories—that's what he really wants—and then see if you can get him to just go that little extra for us."

Bat scowled but said, "Oh, all right. I'll give him a couple of hours."

"Good," Clint said, "then we can meet back at the hotel in, say, three hours and compare notes."

"Fine."

"Better make it four hours," Clint said, changing his mind. "It'll take us some time to get where we're going."

"Four hours, then," Bat said, "but no more."

"Agreed."

As they looked for two cabs Bat asked, "What do you think McGowan's going to do now?"

"The same thing he's been doing."

"Which is what?"

"Not a hell of a lot."

Clint let Bat take the first cab that came along, and as it clip-clopped away he began to look for one for himself. Before he found one, however, he heard someone call his name, someone who had come out of the police department building. He turned and saw Arthur Pine waving at him.

"Mr. Adams," Pine said, running down the steps toward him.

"Hello, Arthur," Clint said. "Did we get you in trouble?"

Pine looked confused.

"No, sir."

"Oh, I thought that was why McGowan had pulled us in to give us a hard time."

"No, sir, not at all. Could we, uh, talk somewhere?"

"Sure, Arthur," Clint said. "What about?"

"Not here," Pine said. "There's a small saloon around that corner and two blocks from here. Could you meet me there in ten minutes?"

That would cut into his fours hours, but maybe not a lot.

"Okay, Arthur," he said. "Ten minutes."

Pine looked around, as if afraid they'd be seen together, but if that was the case why had he yelled Clint's name out? The young man had a lot to learn about being surreptitious.

"Ten minutes," Pine said again, and ran back to the building.

THIRTY-SIX

Clint walked around the corner and down to the saloon he thought Pine meant. There was another that he passed first, but that was probably too close to the police station.

He entered the saloon, which was empty at that time of day. Armed with a beer, he took a back table and waited. Fifteen minutes later Pine walked in, looking as though he had run the two blocks. During the fifteen minutes two other men had entered separately. One was standing at the bar, and the other was sitting at a table. Pine looked at them and was apparently satisfied that they were not policemen. He walked to Clint's table without stopping at the bar.

"Hey!" the bartender shouted.

Pine turned and said, "Me?" The other two men looked over at him.

"Ya gotta order somethin'," the beefy bartender said.

"Uh . . ." Pine walked to the bar. "Let me have a beer, please."

The bartender drew him a beer and Pine walked with it to Clint's table, spilling a bit on the floor.

Pine sat down and put the beer on the table carefully. Some of it still sloshed over.

"You better drink some of that," Clint said.

Pine made a face.

"It's too early."

"What did you want to talk to me about?"

"You were right."

"About what?"

"About Inspector McGowan." The expression on the young man's face was miserable.

"In what way?"

"He's not trying very hard to catch this Chinatown killer."

"Really."

"You were right," Pine said again. "He says it's just as well they kill each other."

"Who kills each other?"

"*Those* people, he calls them." Pine shook his head. "I don't know if I want to be a policeman anymore."

"Why not?" Clint asked. "You don't have to be a policeman like Inspector McGowan."

"But he wasn't always like this," Pine said. "What if the job made him this way? I don't want to end up like . . . that."

"You don't have to, Arthur," Clint said. "You can be whatever kind of policeman you want to be."

"Can I?" Pine asked. "With a boss like that?"

"Arthur," Clint said, "are you still supposed to be following me?"

"Yes."

"All right, then," Clint said, standing up, "let's go."

"Where?"

"You'll see, Arthur," Clint said, "you'll see."

Bat walked to the end of Ross Alley and knocked on Nok Woo Lee's door. When the slot opened he saw Lee's eyes widen, and then the door opened.

"Mr. Masterson, what a pleasant surprise," Nok Woo Lee said.

"Just call me Bat."

"Well, Bat, you can call me Lee," the man said. "Have you come for that talk?"

"Yes," Bat said, "and a drink, if you have it."

"Of course," Lee said. "Come in, come in."

Bat entered and waited for Lee to lock the door, then followed him down the hall to his living quarters.

"Did you and Mr. Adams go down to the Barbary Coast as I suggested?"

"We did."

"And did you run into Mike Jolly?"

"We did."

"You didn't kill him, did you?"

"We didn't."

"Too bad. Sherry?"

"If it's all you have," Bat said.

"It's very good sherry."

"Fine." Bat hated fancy liquors.

"I did hear something about a shooting in one of Jolly's saloons."

"That was us," Bat said, accepting the small glass of sherry. "We had to shoot a toe off two of his men."

"Their toes?" Lee said, laughing. "How wonderful. Do you do that sort of thing often?"

"We have, in the past," Bat said. "Mostly, in a situation like that, somebody ends up dead." He figured this was the kind of thing Nok Woo Lee wanted to hear.

"Really?" Lee said. "How fascinating. And do you and Mr. Adams work well together?"

"Oh, yes," Bat said, "we can pretty much handle any situation that comes along—that can be handled with a gun, anyway."

"Ah," Lee said, "you're referring to these murders."

"Yes," Bat said. "I was wondering if you'd managed to find out anything about it."

"Not very much," Lee said. "I don't think the killer is Oriental."

"No," Bat said, "I agree with you there."

"Have you crossed paths with this man before?"

"Unfortunately, yes."

"Maybe you'll tell me about it?"

"Yes," Bat said, after a moment, "maybe I should."

THIRTY-SEVEN

Clint entered the offices of the *Morning Call* and asked for Allan Marks, hoping the man wouldn't be down in the morgue again. As luck would have it, he was not.

"We can use my editor's office again," Marks said, when he appeared. "We have a lot to talk about."

"I was hoping we would," Clint said.

He followed Marks into the room and waited while he closed the door. This time Marks did not sit behind the desk, but alongside Clint in a chair. Pine stood to one side.

"Allan Marks, this is Arthur Pine. Arthur's a policeman."

"What's he doing here?"

"He's investigating the murders," Clint said.

"Officer," Marks said.

"Mr. Marks," Pine said. "I've read some of your work, and enjoyed it."

"Well," Marks said, "at least he's got taste."

"What did you find out?" Clint asked.

"You were right about Leadville," Marks said. "They had four murders there before they mysteriously stopped."

"Was that right after Dodge?"

"Yes."

"And after that?"

"I have found three more instances of these kinds of murders," Marks said, "a couple of small towns, but the one that interests me is Denver."

"Denver?" Pine asked.

"Yes," Marks said. "Three years ago there were five murders in Denver that match these, and the killer was never caught."

"And since then?" Clint asked.

"This is the first instance since then."

"What do you know about the Denver murders?" Clint asked.

"Not a helluva lot," Marks said, "but I'll know more soon."

"Why is that?"

"Because I'm going there," the reporter said with a satisfied smile. "I got my editor's okay, and I'll be leaving in the morning."

"That's great," Clint said. "Keep in touch with me and let me know what you find out."

"I will."

"And you'll want to contact a friend of mine there," Clint said. "His name's Talbot Roper."

"The private detective?"

"That's right. He'll be able to open some doors for you."

"That'll be great."

"Here, I'll write down his address."

Clint grabbed a piece of paper off the desk and scribbled Roper's address on it.

"Can you read that?"

Marks read it back perfectly.

"Good. Anything else?"

"I got word that there may be something to find out on the Barbary Coast," Marks said. "Apparently the Chinese whore who was killed was working down there, against Nok Woo Lee's orders."

"I know that," Clint said, and recounted his and Bat's experience down there.

"Three-fingered Mike Jolly is supposed to be deadly," Marks said.

"I suspect he is," Clint said. "He certainly seems to have the Barbary Coast under his thumb."

"Maybe you and Bat were lucky to get away from there alive."

"Maybe we were."

"What about the possibility that Nok Woo Lee killed the girl for going against him?" Marks asked.

"No, for two reasons."

"What?"

"It would be bad for business," Clint said, "and even if he was going to kill her, he wouldn't do it while she was with a customer."

"He would if he was trying to make it look like some crazy did it." Marks started to warm to his subject. "Maybe he killed her, but not the other man."

"You think he's trying to make it look like the same killer?"

"It's possible."

Clint thought a moment, then made a face and said, "I don't like that."

"Why not?"

"Too complicated," Clint said. "I want to concentrate on one killer at a time."

"Okay," Marks said. "You concentrate here and I'll concentrate in Denver."

"It's a deal."

In the lobby, after they left Allan Marks, Pine asked Clint, "What you said about one killer? Do you believe that?"

"I believe in keeping things simple, Arthur," Clint said. "To start thinking that there may be a second killer involved just complicates things."

"And what if it turns out that there are two killers?" Pine asked.

"Don't ask, Arthur," Clint said, "just don't ask."

THIRTY-EIGHT

After Clint left Allan Marks, he noticed a telegraph office across the street. Deciding on the spur of the moment he crossed over, went inside, and sent a telegram to Denver. Then he left Pine there to await the answer and headed back to his hotel.

Clint was the first one to reach the hotel, and he wondered how Bat had gotten along at Nok Woo Lee's. He commandeered a back table in the bar and was nursing a beer when Bat walked in. He stopped at the bar first, got a beer for himself, and came over to the table.

"You were right about Lee," Bat said.

"What was I right about?"

"He just wanted to hear stories," Bat said, "lots of stories."

"And you told him lots of stories?"

"Hell," Bat said, "I even made some up. By the time I left there we were buddies. Hold on." He took a big gulp of beer from the mug. "I've got to wash away the taste of that sherry he drinks." He took another drink.

"Did you find out anything during all that storytelling?"

"Not much," Bat said. "Only that Lee doesn't think the killer is Oriental."

"That never entered our minds."

"No, it didn't," Bat said. "What did you find out?"

First Clint told him about his talk with Arthur Pine.

"Where is young Pine?" Bat asked.

"I left him at the telegraph office."

"Telegraph office?"

Clint went on to tell him about his talk with Marks, and about Denver.

"Denver?" Bat asked, looking puzzled. "Clint, you know how much time I spend in Denver. I never heard about any killings."

"Well, I sent a telegram to Talbot Roper and asked him what he knew about it."

"And that's the reply Pine is waiting for?"

"Yes."

"I don't guess there's a lot left for us to do, is there?"

"Is Lee still looking?"

"Looking and listening, he says, but I don't think that man would do anything that didn't suit his own purpose."

"Maybe not," Clint said, "but the last time I was here he helped me, and I don't know what he got out of it."

"Something," Bat said, "I guarantee you."

They sat in silence for a while, each with their own thoughts.

"Denver," Clint said.

"That's what I'm thinking," Bat said. "We both spend a lot of time in Denver, Clint. If this kind of thing was going on there, one of us would have noticed."

"So you think Marks was lying?" Clint asked.

"Or mistaken."

"Why would he lie?"

"Why, indeed?" Bat asked.

They sat alternately staring at each other and into their beer.

"What *was* that editor's name in Dodge City?" Bat asked.

"How old was he?"

"Where is he now?"

"And what the hell," Clint said, "was his name?"

Allan Marks sat at a table in a saloon not far from the building that housed the *Morning Call*. He watched as the man he was waiting for came in and walked over to him.

"Drink?" Marks asked.

"No."

The man sat down.

"What did Adams want?"

"The same things," Marks said. "He's still asking questions."

"He'll get his answers," the other man said, "soon enough."

"How much longer is this going to go on?" Allan Marks asked.

"Are you getting tired, Allan?"

"N-no," Marks answered tentatively. He didn't want to let the other man know how much he feared him.

"Then don't worry how much longer it's going to go on," the man said. "Just sit back and enjoy it, like I'm doing."

"Uh, okay," Marks said, "fine."

"What did you tell him?"

"That I was going to Denver."

The man froze, and then leaned forward.

"Why did you tell him that?"

"I . . . wanted him to think I was out of town, checking on Denver."

"What is there to check in Denver?"

"I, uh, told him that there were similar murders in Denver a few years ago."

"And you don't think he can check on that?"

"I, uh, didn't think he would—"

"Then you're an idiot."

"But—"

"Shut up," the man said. "You have to stay out of sight now, in case he comes looking for you."

"I, uh, planned to."

"They haven't recognized you yet, have they?"

"No."

"That's good. Now why don't you get me a drink."

"You said you didn't—"

"I changed my mind."

The man watched as Marks stood up and went to the bar. The minute there was any hint of recognition, Allan Marks was as good as dead, in spite of the two men's long association.

The man—the killer—was surprised that Bat Masterson and Clint Adams had not figured out who he was yet. They had not even figured out the involvement of Allan Marks, since Dodge City. He was more than a little disappointed in the two legends of the West.

They were no match for him.

Arthur Pine stood in a doorway across the street from the saloon where Allan Marks was carrying a beer back to his table. He had been standing inside the telegraph office when he saw Allan Marks come walking out, and something told him to follow the man. When Marks went into the saloon, Pine waited until a few other men had gone in, then crossed the street and looked in the window. He saw Allan Marks sitting at a table with another man, but the second man's back was to him. He made a mental note of the clothes the second man was wearing, then went back across the street to wait for him to come out.

It just felt good to be doing something other than following Clint Adams. Maybe Marks was just having lunch with someone, but Pine was determined to follow the other man when he came out and see where he went, no matter how long he had to wait.

THIRTY-NINE

"Pine should have been back by now," Clint said.

"What if Roper is out of town and didn't get your telegram?"

"He always has a girl working in his office," Clint said. "She would have sent a reply."

"What can be keeping him, then?" Bat asked.

"I hope Pine didn't decide to do something on his own," Clint said, frowning.

"We've seen how effective he has been," Bat said, "but what could he be doing on his own?"

"I don't know," Clint said, "but maybe we better go and find out."

They both got up and went out and headed back to the area where the the *Morning Call* building was.

Bat waited outside the telegraph office while Clint went inside.

"Well?" he asked as Clint came out.

"No Pine," Clint said, "but we got a reply from Tal Roper."

"What happened to Pine?"

"The clerk said Pine was waiting for the reply when he suddenly walked out and never came back."

Bat looked up and down the street.

"Maybe he had an attack of guilt and went back to Inspector McGowan."

"He was pretty upset and disappointed in Mc-Gowan," Clint said.

Bat shrugged.

"Maybe that's just what he was telling you."

"You mean he was lying to me, working for Mc-Gowan?"

"It's possible."

"I don't think so," Clint said. "I'm going to look around for him."

"All right," Bat said, "I'll go one way, you go the other."

"Right."

They started to split up and then Bat said, "Hey, wait a minute."

"Yeah?"

"What's Roper have to say?"

"Oh," Clint said, "he's never heard of any murders of this type in Denver, not in the past ten years."

"That makes your Allan Marks a liar," Bat said.

"I guess it does," Clint said. "After we have a look around for Pine, maybe we'd better go back into the *Call* office and ask him about it. He's not supposed to leave town until tomorrow."

"If he's leaving at all."

"Meet me back here in half an hour," Clint said, "and we'll find out."

FORTY

After they split up, Clint started checking doorways and alleys, actually hoping he wouldn't find Pine. He would have preferred that the young policeman had gone back to police headquarters, rather than have him turn up dead someplace. But what if Pine had seen somebody interesting, or suspicious, and followed them? Both Bat and Clint knew how effective he was at following someone.

Clint didn't know how far to go in his search, so he simply turned back after fifteen minutes, since he was to meet Bat in half an hour.

Bat was relieved not to have found Arthur Pine's body in a doorway or an alley and returned to the spot where he was supposed to meet Clint just as Clint was coming down the street the other way.

"Anything?" he asked.

"No."

"Where could he have gone?"

"I guess it doesn't matter, right now," Clint said. "Let's go across the street and see if we can talk to Mr. Marks. He's got some explaining to do."

When they asked for Allan Marks at the office, they were told that he was gone for the day.

"I thought he wasn't leaving until tomorrow?" Clint asked.

The man at the desk shrugged and said, "I don't know about that, mister. I just know he's not here now."

"Maybe we can check his home," Clint said.

"Oh, I couldn't give you his home address."

"I think you could," Bat said, and took out some money. He put it on the desk.

"Hey," the man said, "it would take more than that to make me risk my job—"

"How about this?" Bat asked, and swept back his coat to reveal his gun.

"That would do it," the man said. "Let me write it down for you."

He handed Allan Marks's address over to Clint, who accepted it with a thank you.

"Don't forget your money," Bat said to the man, pointing to the money on the desk.

"Uh, sure," the man said, grabbing the money. "T-thanks."

"Have a drink," Bat said, "on me." He followed Clint out.

That was close.

The killer came out of the alley and stared at Clint Adams's retreating back. He wasn't quite ready to face Clint Adams. Actually, truth be told, he would never be ready to face him head-on. He was certainly no match for the Gunsmith face-to-face. He was smart enough to know that—but he was also smart enough to outsmart both the Gunsmith and Bat Masterson.

He waited until Clint Adams was out of sight and then stepped from the alley. He had first seen the man peering in the window at him and Allan Marks. He hadn't known then that the man was a policeman, only that he had caught the interest of somebody, and he couldn't afford that. He had even less reason to believe that the young man was a policeman when he did such a bad job of following him.

It was laughingly easy to lead the man down this alley, and just as easy to leave him behind. He walked away from the alley now, leaving behind a bloody carcass that was once a young police officer named Arthur Pine.

He wondered when the body would be found, and if it would make the front page of the newspapers. Maybe he should give his favorite newspaper reporter a tip.

FORTY-ONE

Clint and Bat knocked on Allan Marks's door and got no answer. They decided to go down to the first floor and talk to his landlord.

"I don't know nothin' about him leavin' town," the man said. He was a small man with white tuffs of hair circling a pink, bald pate. "If he's leavin' town, he ought to tell me about it."

"Maybe it was a spur-of-the-moment thing," Clint said. "I'm sure he'll let you know."

"Then again," Bat said, "maybe he won't."

As they walked away Bat said, "Why should we cover for the bastard?"

"I guess you're right," Clint said. "If he lied to us, we might as well get him in trouble with his landlord."

"Right."

"Of course," Clint said, "if he's the killer—"

"Jesus Christ!" Bat said suddenly, putting his hand on Clint's arm to stop his progress.

"What is it?" Clint asked.

"Marks," Bat said, "of course."

"Bat, what the hell—"

"That editor's name in Dodge City," Bat said, "it was Mark . . . something."

"Are you sure?"

"I can hear it in my head, Clint," Bat said. "Wyatt went to talk to him, and called him Mark . . . something."

"Mark . . . Allen?"

Bat gave his friend a look.

"Don't you think I'd remember that?"

"Well, then, what was it?"

"Mark . . . something," Bat said, wracking his brain.

"That's a big help," Clint said. He frowned. "I'm trying to think if I ever saw him in Dodge."

"I did," Bat said, "that last night, but if you remember, we were both rolling around in mud puddles. His face was covered in mud, but he was *young*, we know that."

"And it was six years ago."

"Damn."

"The Shinns," Clint said. "Lloyd and his brother. They owned the *Times* in Dodge City. Are they still there?"

"They might be," Bat said.

"Let's send a telegram, then," Clint said. "If they're still there, they'll be able to tell us what that editor's name was, and describe him to us."

"If it's this fella," Bat said, "if it's Allan Marks, then we may have found our killer!" He could not conceal the excitement in his voice.

"And if that's the case," Clint said, "he's been playing games with us—especially me—the whole time I've been here in San Francisco."

"And he's not in Denver now," Bat said, "and probably never has been."

"Leadville," Clint said. "I wonder if he was telling the truth about Leadville."

"Luke would know," Bat said. "While we're at it, let's send him a telegram and ask about these kinds of murders in Leadville."

"Let's get back to our hotel," Clint said. "There's a telegraph office right across the street."

They grabbed the next horse-drawn cab that came by and gave the driver the address of their hotel.

"If he's the killer," Bat said, "he's not going to go back to his rooms."

"No, he'll keep his head low for a while, if only to make us think he's been in Denver."

"If we're lucky," Bat said, "he has no idea that we're onto him."

"How could he?" Clint asked. "No, if he's our man he thinks he's fooled us. He thinks that *we* think he's in Denver."

It sounded a little complicated to Bat, but he thought it sounded about right.

FORTY-TWO

When they got back to the hotel they didn't bother going in. Instead, they went directly across the street to the telegraph office.

First, Bat sent a telegram to Luke Short, who was in New York. Second, he sent one to Dodge City, to the Shinn brothers, hoping that they did still, indeed, own and operate the *Dodge City Times*. With that done, they returned to the hotel to await replies to both telegrams.

When they entered the hotel lobby, they saw Inspector McGowan and two of his men waiting for them.

"This time," Bat said to Clint, "we're not going peacefully."

"Let's see what he wants before we start anything," Clint suggested.

As they approached, the inspector turned to face them. His men adopted a belligerent stance behind him.

"What have you done with Pine?" he demanded.

"What do you mean?" Clint asked.

"I mean no one has seen him all day," McGowan said.

Clint was unsure how to react. Pine had obviously not wanted his superior to know that he was with Clint earlier that day. McGowan's next words, however, solved his dilemma.

"I know he was in your company earlier today, Adams," McGowan said. "I want to know where he is."

"I don't know where he is, Inspector, and that's the truth." He explained that the young man had been with him, and that he had left him at the telegraph office across the street from the *Morning Call* to await a reply.

"The reply came in, but Pine wasn't there," he finished. "We looked around the area and didn't see him. We assumed he had returned to work."

McGowan turned to one of his men.

"I want that area searched thoroughly."

"Yes, sir."

The man left, apparently to put the search in motion.

"If anything has happened to that boy I'll hold you two personally responsible," McGowan said.

"Why us?" Bat demanded.

"Because you've been poisoning his mind against me, that's why."

"Look, Inspector," Clint said, "we don't want anything to happen to Pine either."

"Small comfort, Mr. Adams," McGowan said. "What was he doing with you at the *Morning Call*, anyway?"

"We were talking to Allan Marks."

"About what?"

Clint looked at Bat, who reluctantly nodded.

"Inspector," Clint said, "if you'll give us a few

minutes, I'll explain to you what we think we've figured out.''

"A few minutes," McGowan said, "is all I'll give you.''

Clint went through everything they had discovered, and everything they had surmised. The inspector listened to every word intently.

"I'm not convinced you're right," he said when Clint finished, "but it is odd that Marks would lie to you about Denver—and a twofold lie, at that.''

"What are you going to do?" Bat asked.

"First I'm going to find Pine," McGowan said, "and then I'll question Marks.''

"You'll have to find him, too," Bat said. "He wants us to think he's in Denver, so he's going to be laying low.''

"I'll find him," McGowan said. "That's my job.''

"I hope you find Arthur, Inspector," Clint said.

"I'd better," McGowan said, and stalked off.

"I wonder how hard he'll try?" Bat asked.

"I think he'll try hard for Pine," Clint said, "but I don't know about Marks.''

"Hmm," Bat said.

"Bat," Clint said, "where's the last place you'd look for Marks? The last place you'd expect him to be?''

"Two places," Bat said, "Chinatown or the Barbary Coast.''

"He'd stand out too much in Chinatown," Clint said.

"Then that leaves the Coast.''

"I think so.''

They were about to leave the hotel for the Coast when they remembered the telegrams they'd sent.

"Luke will answer quickly," Bat said. "I'm sure of it."

"All right," Clint said, "let's give it an hour, and then head for the Coast. I think our answers are there."

FORTY-THREE

The reply to both telegrams came within the half hour. Luke Short said that there had indeed been murders in Leadville—three of them, and then the killer disappeared.

As for the second telegram, the Shinn brothers did indeed still own the *Dodge City Times*. They said that they had hired a young editor from the East to try to increase the scope and importance of the *Times*, but that they fired him soon after the murders stopped.

That editor's name was Mark Alby.

"Close enough," Bat said.

"Let's go."

They went outside, hailed a horse-drawn cab, and told the driver to take them to the Barbary Coast.

The driver refused to drive into the Barbary Coast, so they had to get out of the carriage on the outskirts.

"Where do we begin to look?" Bat asked.

"Let's just be seen for a while and see what happens," Clint suggested.

"What will happen is that Three-fingered Mike will come looking for us."

"That'll be his misfortune."

"Are we going to shoot off more than toes this time?" Bat asked.

"I think we'd better."

They wandered about the Barbary Coast for an hour, in and out of bars. They stayed away from the Bucket of Blood, where they had first encountered Mike Jolly, but they knew that he probably owned half the saloons they went into.

"I'm having a problem," Clint said.

"With what?"

"With seeing Allan Marks as the killer."

"Why's that?"

"He doesn't seem the type."

"Who does seem the type to be that kind of killer?" Bat asked.

"I think we're forgetting something."

"Like what?"

"Like the man in Dodge City who twice took us to Chinatown, and then disappeared. Who was he?"

"You have an idea," Bat said. "Why don't you tell me who you think he was."

"I think," Clint said, "he was the killer."

"And what about Marks?"

"I think they were working together."

"To do what?"

"What did the Shinn brothers hire their young editor to do?"

"Build the paper up," Bat said.

"Wouldn't making headlines do that?"

"It should. Wait a minute. You think Marks planned the murders so he'd have something to put in the headlines?"

Clint nodded.

"And got somebody else to commit them."

"And then what?"

"And then lost control of him," Clint said. "The killer went to Leadville, and who knows where after that? We don't know where Marks went after Dodge, only that he ended up here."

"And the killer is here, too," Bat said.

Clint nodded.

"So we're looking for two men?"

"That's what I think," Clint said, "but it's just a theory."

Bat looked around at the street they were walking on.

"This is the perfect atmosphere for this killer," he said. "He'd be right at home here."

They stopped walking and simply looked up and down the street.

"You feel it?" Bat asked.

"Yeah," Clint said. "The son of a bitch is here, somewhere."

FORTY-FOUR

From the window of a room in a fleabag hotel, the killer looked down at the street and saw Clint Adams and Bat Masterson.

"Look who's here," he said.

"Who?"

Allan Marks walked over to the window and looked down.

"What are they doing here?" he demanded. "How could they know—"

"They don't know anything," the killer said. "They're guessing."

"Guessing what?"

"That you're here, and not in Denver."

"How could they—"

"I told you they'd check," the killer said. "They both know people in Denver. By now they know you lied about Denver completely."

"They're looking for me?"

"That's right."

"Wait a minute," Marks said. "Do you mean they think I'm you?"

"That would be my guess."

Both men moved away from the window.

"I'm not going to take the blame for what you've done," Marks said.

"Why not?" the other man said. "You started it all, didn't you? I was supposed to make you a big success in Dodge City."

"You were supposed to kill one person," Marks said, "to give me one big headline—and then you went crazy."

"Crazy is not the word," the killer said.

"It's exactly the word."

"Then let me put it this way," the man said coldly. "It's not a word you want to use around me."

His cold eyes bored into Marks's eyes, and the newspaperman averted his gaze.

"You did it," he said, "you did it all."

"Then why haven't you turned me in?" the killer asked. "Why have you let me kill all these years when the urge came back?"

"I have no control over you."

"You're absolutely right about that."

They both fell silent, and the silence grew awkward. Allan Marks suddenly knew what he had to do to get away from this crazy man, to get him out of his life once and for all, so he couldn't follow him anymore. It was too much to have him find him everywhere he went, from town to town, city to city, job to job, and have it start all over again.

"I'm going for a walk." Maybe he could catch up to Adams and Masterson.

''Where?'' the killer asked.

''Just for a walk.''

Marks walked to the door and opened it, but suddenly it slammed shut and the other man spun him around and pinned him to the door.

''I don't think so.''

FORTY-FIVE

Clint and Bat finally quit the Barbary Coast and returned to their hotel. There was nothing to do but wait for McGowan to let them know if he had found Arthur Pine.

"If Pine's dead . . ." Clint said.

"Do you think he is?"

"I have a bad feeling, Bat."

"Yeah, I know," Bat said. "I have it, too."

"I think I'm going to go to my room to think about this for a while," Clint said.

"Sounds like a good idea," Bat said. "I'm kind of tired, myself. I'd like to just take my mind off this for a few hours and give it a rest."

"I know how you feel."

Both men went upstairs, wishing they could forget about the murders for a while, but doubting that they could.

• • •

Bat entered his room and immediately felt the presence of someone else. He took out his gun and pointed it. The Chinese girl in his bed made a high, squeaky noise and pulled the sheet up to her chin.

"What are you doing here?" he asked.

"L-lee send me."

"For what?"

She smiled shyly and dropped the sheet to her waist. She was naked, and her breasts were small but firm, with brown nipples.

"Lee think you need relax," she said.

Bat's first instinct was to kick her out, but then he looked closer at her heart-shaped face, cupid's bow mouth, and round breasts.

"You know what?" he asked, putting the gun aside. "Lee's right."

The girl in Clint's bed was just as small and perfectly formed, just as naked, and just as persuasive.

"What's your name?" Clint asked.

"Tz'u-hsi."

"Come again?"

"Tz'u-hsi," she said more slowly.

"And can you speak English?"

She nodded.

"Well, or do you use that phony pidgin style?"

"Phony?"

"Well," Clint said, "with some of you it's phony."

"It may be phony," she said in perfect English, "but people expect it—men expect it."

"I don't expect it," he said.

"Then I won't do it," she said.

"I'd appreciate it."

"And I would appreciate it if you would get undressed."

"You don't have to do this, you know," Clint said.

"Lee sent me," she said, as if that explained everything. "Besides, I like my job."

"Are you good at it?" Clint asked

She smiled and said, "Come and find out."

She was very good at it. Clint had been with Chinese women before, so that was nothing new. This one, however, had none of that Chinese reserve, no tentativeness at all. Of course, the fact that she was a whore could have had something to do with that.

The fact that she was a whore also explained why she was able to take his penis into her mouth and so expertly suck him and work him into a frenzy *without* allowing him to finish.

"That's torture," he said as she released him slowly, leaving him wet and still wanting.

She stretched out next to him, spread her legs, and said, "Why don't you torture me for a while?"

He got down between her thighs and did just that, using his tongue and lips to bring her to the brink so that she was moaning and thrashing about on the bed.

"Oooh," she said, a long, guttural sound, "don't you leave me like this, you bastard!"

He smiled up at her and said, "Why not? You left me. . . ."

She looked down at him, her eyes glazed, her mouth slack, and said, "You finish me, mister, and then I'll give you a night you'll never forget! Promise!"

"It's a deal," he said, and happily bent to his task.

Outside the hotel the killer stood in a doorway across the street, closing his eyes, smiling and trying to imagine

what was going on in the rooms of Clint Adams and
Bat Masterson.

What was going on now . . . and what would be going
on soon.

Very soon.

FORTY-SIX

Clint's eyes were closed but he could feel the girl, Tz'u-hsi, moving on the bed, ever so slowly. He opened his eyes just a bit so he could see the knife when it started to descend. Moving quickly he caught her wrist and sat up in the bed.

"Hey!" she said, trying to pull away.

"That's my line," he said.

"Let go—"

Clint pried the knife from her hand. It was an evil-looking blade, small but deadly.

"You just tried to kill me," Clint said. "Are you going to tell me that Nok Woo Lee wanted you to do that, too?"

"He—"

"He didn't send you," Clint said.

"How do you know?"

"Because Lee doesn't give anything away for free,"

175

Clint said, "especially not his girls' services. Who sent you?"

She compressed her lips.

"I'm not going to let go until you tell me," he said. "After you do, maybe we can go back to torturing each other."

"I'm not going to tell you who sent us."

"Us?"

"I'm not—"

He cut her off by closing his fist and clipping her on the jaw. He released her arm then and she slumped to the bed. He grabbed his gun and ran from the room, naked.

"Bat!" he shouted, banging on the door. He didn't bother banging again. He backed up, kicked out, and snapped the door open. He leapt into the room with his gun out and looked at the naked man and woman on the bed.

"You only knocked once," Bat said. "I might have made it to the door if you tried again."

Bat released the girl's wrist and she slumped to the bed, unconscious.

"You knew?" Clint asked.

"Of course," Bat said. "Lee wouldn't give one of his girls away for free."

"You knew that, and you had sex with her first?"

Bat made a show of examining his friend's nakedness and said, "Is this the pot calling the kettle black?"

"I'll tie mine up," Clint said, "and you tie yours up. Then we better get dressed and get outside."

"Right," Bat said. "He's got to be around the hotel somewhere. He wouldn't want to miss this."

"Wait a minute," Clint said, halfway out the door.

"What?" Bat already had one leg in his pants.

Clint came back into the room.

"They were going to signal him when the job was done."

"How?"

"My room overlooks the street," Clint said. "How would you think?"

"The window," Bat said. "Dim the lights, or pass a lamp in front of it."

"The light, I think," Clint said, looking at the gas lamp on the wall. "Dim, bright, dim, bright . . . ?"

Bat stood up.

"It can't be that easy."

"After all these years," Clint said, "maybe it can, huh?"

Bat shrugged and said, "It's worth a try."

They carried both girls to Clint's room and put them on the bed, naked, side by side. That done, Clint went to the gas lamp on the wall and then dimmed it, brightened, dimmed it, and repeated the process several times.

Now all they had to do was sit back and wait to see if they were right.

The killer walked down the hall to Clint Adams's room. He was going to save viewing Bat Masterson's dead body for last. When he reached Clint's door he turned the knob slowly until he was sure the door was unlocked, then turned it all the way and opened it. The first thing he saw was the two Chinese whores he'd hired, lying on the bed side by side, naked.

And that meant . . .

Clint stepped out from behind the door, holding a gun on the killer. The man backed out into the hall and turned to run, but Bat Masterson came out of his room with his gun in his hand.

"It's been a long run, friend," Bat said, "but it's over now."

EPILOGUE

"And who was he?" McGowan asked.

"The man in Dodge City, the one who kept turning up after the murders," Bat said. "He'd lead us to the scene, all in a panic, and then disappear."

"A little man," Clint said, "with big ideas."

"Ideas that were planted by Allan Marks," Bat said, "who at that time was going by the name Mark Alby."

They explained to McGowan about Marks being hired to make the *Dodge City Times* into a bigger newspaper.

"He had big ideas," Clint said, "but they got out of hand."

"The killer decided he liked the killing, and if Marks tried to stop him, he'd give him up."

"He sure didn't look like much when we led him away in shackles," McGowan said.

McGowan was not tall, and yet he'd stood several

inches taller than the killer, whose name they still did not know.

McGowan had come to the hotel early that morning, bearing the news of two deaths—Arthur Pine and Allan Marks. When he had come the night before to arrest the killer and the two girls, he still hadn't known about them. He'd only found out this morning, when both bodies were discovered.

"Pine probably saw something he shouldn't have," the inspector said, "and the killer and Marks probably had a falling-out. He cut both their throats."

"I'm sorry about Pine," Clint said, wondering if the man was going to blame him.

McGowan shook his head.

"It's my fault," McGowan said. "If I'd pursued this case more diligently . . ."

Clint and Bat did not reply. Unfortunately, they agreed with the man.

"Can we leave San Francisco?" Clint asked.

"Yes," McGowan said. They were sitting in the lobby and he stood up. "The killer not only confessed last night, he bragged."

"But he wouldn't give his name?"

"He's still playing games," McGowan said, "but we'll identify him soon enough."

McGowan left and the two friends faced each other.

"I feel foolish," Bat said.

"Why?"

"That little man . . . he made a fool out of me in Dodge."

"And we made a fool out of him last night," Clint said.

"It was pretty easy to lure him up to the hotel room," Bat said, "after all the devious moves he's made over the years."

Watch for

THE CHALLENGE

181st novel in the exciting GUNSMITH series
from Jove

Coming in January!